Granite Publishing Presents

Love Notes

#6

Scottish
Legend

Scottish
Legend

By Sherry Ann Miller

Scottish Legend by Sherry Ann Miller
© Copyright 2007 All rights reserved.
First Edition 2007

Published by:

Granite Publishing and Distribution, LLC
868 North 1430 West
Orem, Ut. 84057
(801) 229-9023   Toll Free (800) 574-5779
Fax (801) 229-1924

Cover Design and Art: Tammie Ingram
Layout: Triquest Book Services

ISBN: 978-1-59936-016-4
Library of Congress Card Control Number: 2007922882

Printed in the United States of America 2007
FC Printing, Salt Lake City, UT

For Lynnette and Lora,
two sisters who have found a special place
in my heart.

May joy and happiness follow you
all the days of your life.

Prologue:

"But, sir, when I signed on, there was no mention of undercover work," Jacey protested.

Director Stevens sat erect, his hands folded on his desk, poised as if considering a war strategy. "Like most agents, you were hired for primary skills that excel beyond the average person's, but those skills have nothing to do with where you are most needed. Because of your recent intense training, I think you'll adapt to your new assignment remarkably well, once you get used to the idea."

Jacey placed one hand on the desk and leaned forward, pleading, "Sir, I cannot stay here in Washington, D.C. It is imperative that I to return to San Francisco because my father is . . . ill."

"Your father is a drunk, Agent Munroe. Accept this assignment, and I will personally guarantee him a room in the finest rehab in the country, effective immediately. By the time you return to San Francisco, he'll be stone-cold sober and learning to cope with his addiction."

Jacey swallowed and considered the offer. She would have put her father into a rehabilitation facility years ago if she could have persuaded him. She knew the Director would be far more convincing. "It is tempting, sir."

"Why do I hear a 'but' in that phrase, Agent Munroe?"

After biting her lip, Jacey confessed, "I'm not certain the agency should jeopardize such an important mission by sending me, sir. I've never been entrusted with an undercover assignment before."

"Agent Munroe," Director Stevens said, opening a file folder containing her application, test performance scores and review statements. "You're overqualified, if anything. You run four miles every day, your self-defense skills are quick and incisive, and you placed in the top ten in every test battery we've thrown at you. You have exactly the skills we need. Besides, you're almost a dead ringer for the Chester woman, right down to the long eyelashes. With contact lenses and a little hair-coloring, no one will be able to tell you apart, not even her own father." The Director pushed back from the desk. "Agent Carrington and his team will take you directly to processing, then accompany you to Scotland. You will be provided with around-the-clock shadowing the entire time you're in Galashiels. You leave immediately." He stood up, indicating the meeting was over.

Nodding in agreement, Jacey swallowed the lump of fear in her throat as she stood to face him. Giving him a hard frown, she said, "My opposition must go on my record, sir. My job description did not include undercover work when I signed on, and had I known beforehand, I may not have accepted my current position."

Director Stevens almost smiled. "When you return from Scotland, you can grow sugar beets, become a belly dancer or start your own crop-dusting service, none of which is my concern. Have a nice flight, Agent Munroe."

Jacey managed to reach the door without collapsing. To her dismay, a tall, lean man in a crisp business suit, accompanied by five strong-armed assistants, waited for her right outside the Director's office in the hallway.

"Lee Carrington," the man said, shaking her hand firmly. "Our plane is waiting, Agent Munroe. This way, please."

Scottish Legend

Chapter One

As the airplane began to cross eastward, over the Atlantic Ocean, Jacey entered the plane's small lavatory and stared in amazement as Katie Chester turned to face her. The resemblance between the two women was remarkable.

Katie gasped, then exclaimed, "Genius! Except for the eyes, you look exactly like . . . *moi.*" Her voice had a nasal twang to it that amused Jacey.

"Give me your cell phone and your purse," said Jacey, ignoring what might have been a compliment. "And hurry. We mustn't take long exchanging clothes."

"Right down to business. I like that." The curly-locked, redheaded woman removed a forest-green leather jacket and matching short skirt, and handed them to Jacey. She also removed a light green tank top and gave it to Jacey.

In return, Jacey undressed and gave Katie her modest wool skirt and sweater, a dainty silk blouse and a pair of sturdy walking shoes. Then, Jacey pulled on the other woman's clothing, fastening the patent leather boots all the way up over her knees while tugging the short skirt down so she wouldn't feel so exposed.

With no elbow room, Jacey scrunched herself against the door where she waited patiently for Katie Chester to finish dressing, trying to keep herself from being bumped and jostled too much.

Katie Chester pulled a nylon net over her hair, securing her curly red locks against her scalp, and pulling them away from her face. Jacey assisted Katie with the adjustments on the shoulder-length, golden-brown wig she'd worn earlier, smoothing it over Katie's head, brushing the ends lightly to make the wig appear more natural.

They stared at one another in amazement. "Hard to believe you're not me," said Katie in a cocky half-smile. "If only Daddy could see me now."

"I trust you realize that preventing your *daddy* from seeing you at all is entirely the point of this mission," Jacey countered, wanting absolute certainty regarding the other woman's intentions.

"I know that, Miss Chester," said Katie, addressing Jacey by her new identity. However, Katie was unable to disguise the twang made of her speech, apparently from a narrowed septum in her nasal passages. "Let's hope he doesn't suspect anything before I testify against him. Otherwise, the consequences for us both could be . . . well, deadly."

"It's good to know we're on the same page," said Jacey. She opened the purse she'd brought with her into the lavatory, gave a passport to Katie and said, "Your name is Veronica Black. Here's your passport and purse. Veronica is a quiet girl, she speaks in a very soft voice, which will disguise Katie's twang a bit. Can you manage that?"

"I have no choice," Katie whispered. "Nice to meet you, Katie Chester." Her resonating voice quivered as she pushed a shoulder bag into Jacey's hands.

"You're certain you want to do this?" Jacey asked for the last time. "Because the moment you walk out that door, you will be Veronica Black for at least a month or two, maybe longer. If you're the least bit hesitant, now is the time to say so."

"It's not a matter of ambiguity," came the twanged response. "If you knew my father, you'd understand it's all about survival."

"Believe me," affirmed Jacey, beginning to feel concerned even more about her new assignment, yet hoping to reinforce Katie's responsibility to never consider herself Katie Chester from that moment on until the mission ended. "I've learned enough about Myles Chester in the past twenty-four hours to last a lifetime." She handed Katie a pair of golden brown contact lenses and waited while Katie put them in her eyes.

Afterward, Katie smiled briefly and shook Jacey's hand. "Good luck, Katie Chester. It was nice meeting you." She turned and opened the lavatory door to exit the small room.

"And you," said Jacey, closing the door behind the new Veronica Black.

Fumbling with a pair of green contact lenses until she managed to insert one in each eye properly, Jacey lifted her head and looked at herself in the mirror. She hardly recognized the woman who stared back from the glass. Short, curly, red locks coiled at odd angles around her head, deep green eyes the color of rich emeralds, and her clothes – forest-green, patent leather boots, skirt and jacket, and a revealing tank top – all gave

Jacey the appearance of a stranger. The dramatic changes also gave her courage.

Katie Chester was known for her flamboyant, flirtatious behavior, attributes foreign to Jacey's reserved, yet professional manner. If she could let herself relax, this might be a fun adventure, playing the role of a wealthy, impudent, spoiled heiress.

The twelfth of June and it begins, she worried as she made her way toward a seat beside Lee Carrington, who had been sitting by Katie before Jacey had escaped to the ladies' room. She noticed Katie Chester, who now looked remarkably like Jacey Munroe, was now seated in the middle of an eight-man team that had joined Jacey's escort of six men when they boarded. It was the same seat where Jacey had been sitting only a few minutes before. The real Katie Chester, now known as Veronica Black, would be escorted back to a Washington, D.C., safehouse within a few days of her arrival in Edinburgh, Scotland.

Meanwhile, Jacey Munroe, disguised as Katie Chester, would travel from Washington, D.C., to Edinburgh, Scotland by air, and then to Galashiels, Scotland, by passenger train, where she would spend the next month or two at the manor of Master Matthew Forbes, a business associate of Myles Chester. Master Forbes had entertained the real Katie Chester only once before, when she was seven years old. Because of his unquestionable loyalty to Lord Chester, Master Forbes had accepted his Lordship's assignment of entertaining Katie while her father went on trial in Washington, D.C., for securities fraud, treason and first-degree murder. Myles Chester still had no idea that his daughter, Katie, intended to testify against him, nor that she had compelling evidence to present.

Fear started to seep slowly into Jacey's stomach as she sank beside Agent Lee Carrington and twisted her legs into a most unbecoming posture, one she had seen Katie use several times already during their flight. "Ready for that bad boy attitude I crave?" she teased, picking up the thread of conversation Katie had left behind.

"Ma'am," Lee snorted with a hearty laugh, "I doubt you can handle someone feisty as me, but since you like to fight fire with fire . . . ." He teasingly pulled her toward him, and kissed her eagerly in front of everyone aboard the plane.

* * * * *

For a brief moment, Jacey paused to study her reflection in the translucent glass snugged into the front door. *Appalling*, she decided, and hoped she would find something less risqué within the confines of the seven suitcases the chauffeur was now hauling from the limousine and stacking onto a rolling luggage rack.

Glancing heavenward, she whispered, "Dear God, forgive me for what I am about to do, and please let it all work out for the best."

Before she could utter a quick *amen* the heavy oak and glass door whisked open and a petite, silver-haired woman shook her hand vigorously.

"Katherine, me child! How ye've grown! Come in. Come in. Master Forbes is expectin' ye."

"Thanks, Miriam. I can't wait to see him, either," Jacey responded, but no amount of practice made her voice twang quite as much as Katie's had.

The woman smiled warmly, her brown eyes alive with amusement. "I thought ye wouldn't be remembering me, Katherine. Ye were only a wee lass when ye were here last."

"Of course," said Jacey. "But, could you drop the Katherine? Everyone calls me Katie these days."

"If it pleases ye," the woman hesitated with uncertainty. "How be it, Lord Chester still refers to ye as– "

"Only because he is my father," Jacey interrupted. "Certainly not because he is my friend, sending me off to Scotland like so much baggage." She hoped the woman heard bitterness in her voice, and a certain edge of callous disregard.

"Wait in the parlor, Miss Katie. I'll fetch Master Forbes straight away."

Jacey nodded and entered the room on the left as indicated by Miriam Westly who retreated deep into the house. Now, the true test would come. If Jacey passed this one successfully, all would work out well for her in Galashiels, Scotland. If she failed, it could cost the fortunes, perhaps even the lives, of many.

Swallowing a lump of fear that had gathered in her throat, Jacey felt grateful for a moment's reprieve before she had to face Master Forbes. If she could fool him, she could deceive anyone.

Her thoughts were interrupted when the front door opened. She heard two people enter, then the door slammed shut, the glass rattling in the frame.

From the foyer, an angry man shouted, "If ye think for one minute I'd be spending the next month playing escort to a lovesick little goose, ye are mistaken!" His voice chilled Jacey all the way through to her spine.

"But Rob," soothed a woman with honey-sweet tones, "You promised you'd repay my favor. And maybe it won't be for a whole month. The trial could be over in three weeks."

"That promise was extracted under duress and ye knew it," the man insisted.

His deep voice grated on Jacey's nerves, sending tremors of fear through every fibre. She tip-toed toward the entrance, keeping to the right of the door, so she wouldn't be detected.

"I don't like this anymore than you do, darling," the woman coaxed. "But, we have to follow Lord Chester's instructions to the letter if Uncle Matthew is to stay in his good graces. Imagine the financial disaster the entire village would suffer if Lord Chester withdrew his support from the woolen mill."

"Myles Chester may own your uncle," the man reminded. "He'll never be owning me."

"All right," the woman said, her voice faltering with emotion. "I didn't want to use this against you, Rob, but you leave me no choice. If you refuse to help, I will go straight to your aunt and tell her the truth behind your divorce."

The man named Rob thundered. "Ye could do something so dastardly?"

For a brief moment, silence fell upon the entry hall, then Rob yelled, "Why, ye selfish little–"

"I relent, Rob," the woman interrupted. "But, how can you refuse this one simple favor? Katherine Chester would succumb to your charms in a minute. All you have to do is help her forget about her boyfriend in America. When she finally leaves Forbes Manor, she'll have her confidence restored. It's not like we're asking you to do anything immoral."

"Which is another point I don't understand," Rob argued. "Why would Chester send his daughter all the way to Scotland on a lark to get her away from a boyfriend? According to the tabloids, they seem to be crawling out of the woodwork wherever she goes."

Expelling her breath, Jacey was surprised to realize she'd been holding it. Myles Chester had evidently given the Forbes a false reason why Katie would be their houseguest. It angered her. How dare these two strangers bargain over Katie as though she were a piece of meat at the butcher? Her facade melted completely as her own emotions swelled to the surface.

The man cursed and demanded, "How do ye propose that I manage a spoiled little wretch like Miss Katherine Chester?"

Jacey's fiery temper got the better of her with that remark and, without giving her actions a second thought, she burst into the hall and gave the man a freezing glare that would have crystalized the heart of a polar bear. "It's Katie!" she snapped. "And how dare you call me a spoiled little wretch when you've never even met me!"

For a moment, surprise registered on Rob's face as he realized he had been overheard. Their eyes locked and a brisk, insufferable tension filled the great hall.

Before Rob had a chance to respond, Jacey said, "Now, if you'll excuse me, I'll –"

"Katherine!" came a jovial voice behind her.

Jacey swallowed and slipped on a mask of indifference before she turned, fists clenched at her sides. "Uncle Matthew," she said brightly. "Oh, it is all right to call you Uncle, isn't it?" she asked, planting a kiss upon the older man's cheek.

The stout, balding gentleman embraced her in a quick hug. "Of course. In fact, I prefer it. Your father and I are close as brothers, as you know." He laughed and his protruding stomach jiggled with the effort. "And you have changed to Katie? I should have known. The newspapers and magazine articles all identify you as Katie now, don't they?" It was more statement than question.

Turning to his other guests, Master Forbes wrapped a stocky arm around Jacey's waist and pivoted her to meet them. "Robert Roy McLennan, Rachel, meet Katie Chester. Rob is an old friend of our family. Rachel, as you know, is my niece." A flicker of emotion crossed Master Forbes' beady eyes as he noticed Rachel wipe a stray tear from her cheek.

For a few silent moments, Jacey waited and watched. Rachel was exactly as described, with soft, brown hair and wide, dark brown eyes. Rachel was thin, almost gaunt. Her leanness did not, however, detract from her stirring beauty.

Although Rachel was tall for a woman, Robert Roy McLennan towered above her. He stood at least six-foot-four inches, with broad, well-muscled shoulders and arms, a slim waist and not a scrap of fat on him anywhere. Jacey could almost feel the electric current that emanated from Rob McLennan, who was slowly simmering with anger.

Successfully, Jacey controlled the trembling of her knees as Rob's watchful blue eyes, framed by auburn hair, surveyed her appearance. Jacey felt oddly discomfited, knowing how she looked did not suit her true personality. His eyes missed nothing, however, and she forced herself to strike an alluring pose just as she knew Katie would, then she turned her attention back to Rachel.

"Yes, Rachel. I thought I recognized you." Jacey held out a hand and shook Rachel's quickly, avoiding the mocking smile that seemed to be forming around the firm line of Rob's mouth.

Then, dismissing the couple before her with a brief nod of her curls, she turned her attention to Master Forbes, ignoring the introduction to Rob McLennan completely. "Now," she asked with coy deliberation, "what was my father telling me about the stables? I seem to recall a horse named Chestnut, is that right?"

The robust Matthew Forbes nodded. "He passed, I'm afraid. But, he sired a few excellent geldings, fairly docile, perhaps one of those might catch your interest."

She gave him a conspiratorial grin and shook her head.

Master Forbes pivoted her around, his hand at the small of her back, and winked knowingly. "We have a magnificent stallion, one you'll be able to challenge."

Leading her down the hall, through the massive kitchen and out the back door, he escorted her along a tree-lined path toward the stables. "You were at Girl's Camp the last time your father was here, as I recall. He told me they had several horses, real champions. We couldn't hope to compete for your favor when you had a corral full of your favorites to choose from, now could we?"

"I don't suppose my father told you there was a Boy's Camp less than a mile from ours?" she asked, forcing a mischievous expression.

"No," Master Forbes laughed heartily, his dark eyes dancing with delight. "You were always the one to enjoy a casual flirtation."

Just as abruptly as his laughter began, a serious expression crossed his face. "But, this matter of your father sending you off to Scotland to get you away from an ardent admirer. Really, Katie, I certainly do not approve. And, in the middle of his trial." His voice held just enough censure to sound convincing.

"Neither do I," she agreed.

"Not that I don't respect Lord Chester," he hastened to add. "But, I suppose with his keen business sense he regards you as," he paused, "an investment."

"His one prize possession," Jacey admitted. "He's about to discover I'm not an artifact to be guarded jealously. I belong to myself."

"Well said," he complimented, his plump body short of breath at the distance they traveled to the stables. "I admire you, Katie. Regardless of all the obstacles in your path, you've turned out remarkably well. Most of the rich are not so fortunate. Their money dominates . . . to the exclusion of all else."

"Oh, don't think I don't enjoy wealth, Uncle Matthew. It's just that I enjoy my little games more," she teased.

Having reached the stables, Master Forbes unbolted the lower door and held it open for Jacey. She stepped inside and swept past each stall, looking for the perfect stallion. She found him in the third stall back on her left. A gorgeous, chestnut animal with gleaming muscles and sinewy legs. She grabbed some sugar cubes from a bag by the gate and held them out to him with her hand.

"He's beautiful," she murmured. "What's his name?"

"Storm," said Master Forbes. "Would you like to ride him?"

Thinking how she would look astride Storm in the outfit she wore stopped Jacey cold. "I think I'll wait until I'm dressed more appropriately for riding," she decided.

Master Forbes laughed. "You do like to dress up for every occasion. Perhaps you also remember that dinner is a formal affair?"

"Of course," she smiled, stroking the magnificent horse with her hands. *At least this is one Storm I can handle.*

Chapter Two

Jacey could scarcely eat the delicious food Miriam had prepared for their dinner. Having been briefed on all the household staff by Lee Carrington on the plane from Washington, D.C., to New York, after getting her hair cut, permed and colored to match Katie Chester's, Jacey cringed, knowing Miriam would be disappointed. Her lack of appetite had nothing to do with Miriam's extravagantly prepared cuisine, but rather, it was the unsettling way Rob McLennan's eyes danced her direction throughout the meal. The revealing dinner gown Jacey had found among Katie's clothing selections seemed to have caught Rob's attention, and Katie felt self-conscious and uneasy wearing it. Small talk about the weather back in New

York, her flight to Edinburgh, and guarded questions about Myles Chester's trial, did nothing to relieve her discomfort.

Since returning from the stables, Rob seemed determined to cling to every word she spoke. Disconcertingly, he had apparently agreed to fulfill his promise to Rachel, regardless of his protestations earlier in the day.

Finally, the strain of his unwanted observation flared her temper. She glared ominously at Rob, then turned her attention to Master Forbes. "I must ask you, Uncle Matthew, to release Mr. McLennan from his promise to accompany me while I am here in Galashiels."

Fear stamped its way across Master Forbes' face as plainly as if she'd threatened him. Rachel's brown eyes screamed their silent plea, *Please, Katie, don't say anymore.* But, it was Rob's challenging look that mocked her. Had Rob known her better, he would never have allowed his *I dare you!* expression to surface. Silently, Jacey wondered how Rob would react if he knew her true identity as an FBI agent.

Master Forbes wiped his mouth with a napkin, choked a moment on a piece of brisket, then composed himself and gave her a meek, "Oh?"

"I have no need for an escort service," she insisted, glancing at Rob with censure. "It seems Mr. McLennan was invited to chaperone me, but I find his company most disagreeable . . . and he apparently shares my discomfort. Besides, I made prior arrangements for an escort of my own choosing."

"Not that scoundrel your father told me about?" asked Master Forbes, beads of perspiration forming on his forehead. "He did not follow you to Scotland, did he?" His color changed from robust pink to chalk white in a matter of seconds.

His anxiety touched Jacey, softening her heart towards him. Rob, however, remained unfazed at her announcement, and this bothered her more than his staring at her all evening.

"No," she smiled reassuringly. "I wasn't all that fond of Derek. My father told him that if he made any attempt to see me again, I would be cut out of Father's will with lightning speed. And, with that same rate of acceleration, Derek vanished." She sighed to indicate how bored she was with the topic, her performance for Rob's eyes alone. Allowing her expression to take on a dream-like quality, she sighed wistfully toward Rob and said sweetly, "I met the most wonderful man on the flight to Edinburgh. He has business dealings in Galashiels and he plans to remain in the area for a few weeks. I promised to picnic with him tomorrow. That is," looking back at Master Forbes, "Uncle Matthew, if I may have your permission." Flashing her bright green contact lenses at him, she slanted her long, dark lashes seductively.

The color returned immediately to Master Forbes' cherubic features. "Of course, my dear. In fact, I encourage you to make the acquaintance of several young men in the area." He chuckled in obvious relief. "Variety is the spice of life and all that," he said, giving her a tooth-filled smile and patting her hand paternally.

Jacey stifled the urge to roll her eyes. Instead, she glanced at Rob, who almost seemed amused with her antics, and insisted, "As long as I do the choosing, Uncle Matthew. I think that is something Mr. McLennan and I can both agree upon."

For a fraction of a second, a scowl stamped its way across Rob's handsome face, then vanished. Giving her a guarded, but polite smile, Rob nodded his head in compliance.

By the time Jacey reached her bedroom, she was trembling. Stepping into the adjoining bathroom, she ran cold water over her face, then studied her reflection in the mirror. Frowning, she decided she hated her new hairstyle. "I look like Orphan Annie! How did I ever let myself get talked into this?" she asked the stranger in the mirror as she pulled at a curl and watched it spring back into place.

Suddenly, a car engine roared to life below her open bedroom window. Jacey stepped to the curtain and watched as Rachel bent over the window well of Rob's Landrover, apparently to kiss Rob McLennan goodbye. A painful twinge settled in Jacey's abdomen. However, Rob's hands did not leave the steering wheel, nor did he seem particularly interested in Rachel's kiss. This gave Jacey small comfort. She dismissed her own physical reactions as tension, exacerbated by Rachel's obvious affection for a man Jacey disliked.

Jacey noticed one of the maids had already pulled the bedding down on her four-poster bed. Then, she heard a knock on the bedroom door. She slipped between the bed sheets and placed her head upon the pillow. When settled, she asked sleepily, "Who is it?"

"It's Rachel. May I come in?"

"Yes," Jacey replied, forcing a smile upon her face.

The door opened hesitantly. Rachel stepped inside and closed the door behind her. "I'm sorry, Katie," she said, squeezing her hands together nervously, "for what we said in the hall, earlier today. I've been miserable about it all evening."

"No need to apologize," Jacey responded. "No harm done."

Rachel approached the bed and sat timidly upon it, taking Jacey's hand in hers. "You see, Katie, Uncle Matthew's woolen mill had a setback a few years ago when the sheep developed a form of mad cow disease. Over six hundred animals had to be culled. Your father's business loan is the only thing keeping the mill going right now. If he were to call the loan due, we'd be bankrupt. Uncle and I thought if we could replace your heartthrob with someone your father might approve, he might dismiss the interest on the loan." She sighed. "It seems so foolish now, in retrospect."

"Especially in view of the fact that you're in love with Rob, yourself," observed Jacey.

"Me? Love Rob?" Rachel asked with a look of surprise.

Jacey grimaced, then confessed, "It seems I mistook your kiss goodnight for something more."

"You were watching?" Rachel asked in astonishment.

"He gunned his engine and it surprised me," Jacey explained. "I went to the window to see what the noise was all about."

"You angered Rob at dinner," Rachel admitted. "And kissing him was just my way of teasing him back into a better mood. You know, the Scottish legend."

"The Scottish legend?" asked Jacey.

"You don't remember," she said, shaking her head. "You were probably too young last time you were here."

"I was only seven, then," agreed Jacey, nodding.

Rachel smiled, as though wondering where to begin. "Centuries ago, a McLennan clansman fell in love with a woman from a rival clan. Their fathers refused them permission to marry. Obediently, they married others. Unfortunately, their marriages brought neither o them happiness. According to legend, no McLennan since that day has ever had a happy marriage. The Scottish legend claims that until the two clans are united through wedding vows, the McLennans are doomed to marital misery."

Jacey shook her head. "It sounds like half the marriages in America."

Rachel nodded in agreement.

"Did I hear correctly earlier today? That Rob is divorced?"

"Yes, four years ago. He told his wife he couldn't father children and she left him. She married shortly afterward and has two children from her second husband."

"He's divorced and he's sterile."

"I guess so." Rachel shrugged.

"And, he's a living Scottish legend in these parts. What a reputation to live up to." Jacey almost felt sorry for Robert Roy McLennan, but remembering some of his smug expressions at dinner, she returned to her previous feelings toward him.

"I was sorry to hear that you broke up with Derek," offered Rachel, changing the subject.

"As I said at dinner, I'm not all that lovesick. I'm just disappointed there are so few men around who are not fortune hunters."

Agreeing with a nod, Rachel said, "You've changed so much since you were a child, Katie. I can't get over it."

"How so?" Jacey asked, arching an eyebrow.

Bowing her head, Rachel confessed, "You were rather spoiled when you were younger. You threw tantrums every time you didn't get your way. I couldn't wait to send you home."

Jacey frowned. "Was I that horrible?"

Rachel nodded. "I wouldn't bring it up at all, but I wanted you to know I like the Katie you've become."

"I apologize for my childhood behavior," said Jacey. "I wouldn't want you to think poorly of me."

"I don't, honestly. Would you tell me why your father doesn't want you with him during his trial?" Rachel asked.

Jacey sighed, unsure where to begin, nor how much to tell. Rachel was Master Forbes' niece, having been raised by him, and loved him dearly. How much should she share? How much would get back to Myles Chester? Weighing cause and effect, she finally answered, "I don't approve of some of his business methodology. We had a disagreement, he didn't like what I had to say, so he shipped me off to Scotland."

"You must have been very bold to disagree with him. In Scotland, women are taught 'tis better not to disagree with those in authority, especially our fathers. 'Tis better to let the men concern themselves over our welfare."

"Have no fear," warned Jacey. "My father's concern for me is shallow, Rachel. My being out of the country only makes me unavailable to his enemies. Don't think for one moment all of this has anything to do with his undying love for me."

"You honestly feel that way?" Rachel asked, her brown eyes widened in disbelief.

Jacey tried to explain. "My father's motto is do unto others before they get the chance. I can't live that creed."

"That's why you've shortened your name to Katie?" Rachel surmised. "It's part of your rebellion against him."

"Something like that," Jacey nodded. "Since we're both eager to appease my father over this compulsory vacation, why don't we let bygones be bygones? I really could use a friend in this castle."

"Gladly." Rachel hugged her. "But, I don't know that Rob is as forgiving as I am. He was upset over what he calls your 'flippant attitude' at dinner tonight. I don't think he trusts you."

"Nor I, him," admitted Jacey.

"He's so stubborn," Rachel complained. "When he gets focused on something, he doesn't give up until he completely understands it."

Which may make my mission impossible, worried Jacey.

Rachel stayed to visit until nearly one in the morning. Finally, around two a.m., Jacey sensed the household was asleep except for herself. She dialed Lee from her satellite phone, and he answered on the first ring.

"Why weren't you wearing your bug at dinner?"

"You should have seen the dress I had to wear," she complained. "There was no place to put it where it wouldn't show through the fabric. Dinner is formal at Forbes Manor, and Katie packed nothing modest enough to hide the smallest transmitter."

"All right. That's a problem we'll solve tomorrow with some other dresses. We can arrange for them to arrive from the airport as lost luggage. In the meantime, keep that bug on you at all times."

"Yes, sir," Jacey agreed. "But, send me a pair of sweats or something I can run in that doesn't scream out for attention, will you?"

Lee laughed. "You don't care for chartreuse?"

"Or fuchsia," she added. Then, changing the subject, Jacey asked, "Did we get the helicopter?"

"Yes, and plenty of audio and visual coverage for you, so don't go walking around your bedroom in the nude."

Jacey smiled. She didn't know whether to be worried or relieved.

"Next," said Lee, "stay on track. Katie sleeps in every morning, she's never the first to arise. Always be the last down to breakfast. I'll be arriving at Forbes Manor around noon. Remember to greet me like we discussed."

"Of course. But, Lee, you know it's just the job. I don't have any of those feelings for you."

"You've made that abundantly clear, Agent Munroe." Lee's voice seemed to have an edge to it.

Tackling the subject they'd ignored, she said, "What am I supposed to do about Robert Roy McLennan?"

"We're running his records," Lee said. "I should know something before I come over to-morrow. Why don't you invite Mr. McLennan to picnic with us? Rachel could come with us, too."

"I doubt he'll come, but I'll try," she said, though Jacey held out little hope Rob would ever agree, especially after she'd snubbed him at dinner.

After they hung up, Jacey felt grateful she had Lee Carrington as her team leader. Now, she had one friend inside the castle and one without. And, Robert Roy McLennan to keep Jacey on her guard.

Chapter Three

The following morning, being in a kinder mood, Jacey accepted Rachel's challenge to a game of tennis. Better still, Rob McLennan had telephoned to invite the Forbes, Jacey, and Lee to dinner at McLennan Hall the next evening. Did the invitation mean Rob had forgiven Jacey for her behavior last night?

A niggling doubt reminded Jacey about Rachel kissing Rob in the driveway. Perhaps Rob wanted to invite only Rachel, but did not want to appear rude to her houseguest. Jacey refused to analyze why this thought bothered her.

On the tennis court, Rachel's backhand wickedly lobbed the ball across to Jacey, but she did her best to keep up. In the last set, Rachel slammed the ball over the net and Jacey ran backwards to catch it. Leaping in the air, she swung her racquet high, but missed the ball in the short space it would take to dangle off the edge of a dime. She turned around just in time to watch the ball hit inside the left corner of the court and bounce off the pavement into a thick hedge.

Jacey had to get down on her knees and stretch far into the prickly bush in an effort to retrieve it, but she couldn't quite reach the ball without scratching herself on the brambles. Knowing the real Katie Chester would refuse to even try, she hesitated.

Suddenly, denim-clad legs were standing next to her and a familiar voice said, "Here, let me."

Jacey looked up, way up into Rob's hypnotizing blue eyes. His offer of assistance brought questions to Jacey's mind. If she refused his offer, he would say, "Spoiled rich girls always get their way." On the other hand, if she allowed him to retrieve the ball, he could say, "Spoiled rich girls can't do anything." Jacey frowned.

"Come now," he chided, getting down on his knees beside her. "I won't bite. Your arm isn't long enough to reach the ball." He stretched his hand through the thick hedge beside her, which brought his chest almost parallel to hers.

"I'll help you." Her response was a compromise.

Spoiled little wretch, am I? Jacey fumed silently as she moved her hand alongside Rob's and reached the ball at the same time, regardless of the prickly thorns that scratched and stung her forearm. Unfortunately, this action also brought her chest to virile chest with Rob. Silence enveloped them as they pulled the ball slowly out of the brambles together.

Jacey's eyes widened as her vision wandered from Rob's strong hand, clutching half the ball, to his well-muscled arm sprinkled with fine, dark hair, to the V of his riding jacket, which she now noticed was open, his muscles straining against the fabric of a cotton shirt. Dismayed at the emotions tumbling inside her, Jacey found her eyes transfixed upon his firm, inviting lips. For reasons she did not understand, she wanted to reach out and touch his lips with her fingertips, but she refused to heed the temptation.

"I believe I will take it back," Rob said in a hoarse whisper.

"What?" Jacey asked, forcing her vision from his lips up to his clear, sky-blue eyes.

"Ye don't have to prove a point," he said. "I don't think ye are all that spoiled. Rich? Probably. But, not spoiled."

"Oh?" Jacey questioned, smoldering flames igniting deep inside at their nearness. Her heart beat erratically inside her chest, she felt flushed and incapable of saying another word to him.

"Your hands," he explained, stroking the back of her fingers upon the ball, apparently undisturbed by the close contact of their bodies. "Your hands are the hands of a woman who has known work in her life."

"Oh?" Jacey asked once again, powerless under his scrutiny.

"Manicured nails, neat and trim, no heavy lacquer. Your veins are visible," he said, releasing his hold on the ball, letting it rest in her hand. Meanwhile, he methodically stroked the pale blue streak on the back of her hand with the tip of his finger.

Jacey felt hot fire spread from the caress and surge up her arm, engulfing her in a sensation much stronger than mere desire.

Unexpectedly, Rob stood up and pulled her to her feet. "A spoiled child sees little work," he said. "Her nails are long, like daggers."

The movement from half crouching to standing up started her circulation again. Fortunately, Jacey found a small cache of strength left within her.

"Apology accepted," she whispered, surprised at the huskiness in her voice.

"Thank you," he smiled, a teasing sparkle in his eyes. "I guess that calls for a kiss."

Before she could protest, he bent his head and captured her lips with his. The contact made her lower abdomen knot tightly. Her heart danced with excitement. At the same moment, screeching alarms sounded in her brain and she was vaguely aware of her hands pressing against his chest.

When he finally released her, Jacey gasped. "Really, Mr. McLennan!"

"'Tis Rob," he interrupted casually. "Really what?"

"One apology does not entitle you to fringe benefits," she scolded.

"I could apologize once more and try again," he suggested, his lips curving into a broader smile.

In answer to his suggestion, Jacey turned quickly away and stomped back onto the court, praying her knees would not buckle. Rachel met her at the net.

"I forgot to warn you. Rob is impetuous," she laughed.

"Thanks a lot," Jacey grumbled, handing her the ball.

Rachel waved at Rob. "We'll be finished in a minute. Why don't you go on up?"

He smiled, waved and turned toward Forbes Manor, then walked toward the back door.

"I'm just as surprised as you are," Rachel confessed when Rob was out of hearing range. "Rob isn't one to openly display affection. Not like you, I mean."

"Like me?" Jacey asked.

"We've seen the photos," Rachel confessed. "We get quite a few press releases this far from the busy metropolis. You forget, Katie, that your father's money nearly owns this town. We even have a DVD of you running through the airport and jumping up into the arms of that Naval Officer . . . you had us women drooling. You're lucky to be able to display affection so easily in public like that."

It was a bold reminder to Jacey. She wasn't supposed to react like herself, she was supposed to put on a show just as Katie Chester would if she were here.

By the time they had reached the kitchen door, Rob was already inside, sitting at the table with a tall glass of lemonade in his hand.

"Miriam said she'll pack a lunch for all four of us. What do you say, Katie? Shall we make it a foursome?" he asked.

It took a few seconds for Jacey to realize he was speaking to her. "With Lee?" She hoped her voice sounded anxious enough. "Is he here?"

"In the parlor. I put him to work on some old Forbes family records. Seems your Lee is quite a history buff," explained Rob.

Still dismayed at her unsettled reaction to Rob's nearness and his kiss on the tennis court, Jacey plastered a big smile of pretense on her face. "Hold that thought," she giggled. "I'll go speak with Lee about the picnic."

Turning toward the kitchen door, she called, "Lee! Lee! Are you really here?"

"In the hall," came his loud response. Apparently, he'd been waiting to hear her come in so they could make a grand display, as they'd discussed.

Jacey waited until Lee pushed the door open and stood in the doorframe to the kitchen before racing around the table and into his open arms, kissing him affectionately all over his face until he captured her lips with his and lingered there.

When he finally let her up for air, she gushed, "I'm so glad you came! I've missed you so!"

Laughing, he tucked her next to his side and teased, "It's been almost a whole day we've been apart."

"Let me look at you," she said, facing him. "Yes, yes, it's really you."

"And if my lips are not deceiving me, you must be Katie Chester, my little sleepy-head on the train," he bantered.

"I didn't sleep that much," she protested, punching him playfully in the arm.

"Fiery, too," Lee grinned. "I had no idea you had such a temper. Perhaps you should have warned me between naps." His gray eyes sparkled with mischief.

Wrapping her arms around his neck, she challenged, "Sleepy, fiery and more."

"She's a handful, that's certain," came Rob's voice behind her.

Jacey moaned, "Oh, Rob. I'm so sorry. Were you properly introduced?"

"We introduced ourselves," Lee nodded.

"We did, and I asked Lee if he would consider bringing Rachel and me on your picnic today." Rob gave her a defiant glare.

"Your decision, Katie," said Lee. "I'll remain neutral on this one."

Jacey looked up into Rob's challenging blue eyes. It seemed as though he was daring her once again! She should make him sweat this one out a little, she decided. He was entirely too confident. "Well," she began, "I thought we could go alone."

"Until I kissed ye," Rob said unexpectedly. Directing his remarks to Lee, he continued, "Sorry to disappoint, Lee, but Katie and I hit it off quite well today, and now the poor lass doesn't know how to tell ye she would love nothing more than a picnic for four."

"That's not true!" Jacey protested. "I didn't kiss you. You –"

"Come now," Rob chided. "As Rachel is my witness, ye responded more than generously to me. Isn't that true, Rachel?"

By this time, Rachel was standing beside Rob, and apparently shocked by his arrogant behavior.

"Wait a minute," Lee said with finality. "Katie, did Mr. McLennan kiss you, or did he not?"

"Well, I . . . Yes!" she snapped, her green eyes flashing daggers at Rob. "He certainly did!" Her voice echoed the anger she felt at this ridiculous conversation.

"Very well," Lee said, his voice cooling down quickly. "If you want Rob and . . . ," his eyes rested upon Rachel's face, "and Rachel to join us, you shouldn't be afraid to say so."

"I'm afraid of nothing!" Jacey said crossly, wondering just how far Lee was prepared to take their starring roles. "Fine, let them come."

"It's nice to meet you, Mr. Carrington," said Rachel, shaking Lee's hand. "Why don't I show you the arboretum," she suggested, responding to Rob's nodding his head toward her and Lee, and in one quick gesture she took Lee's hand and led him from the room.

When they were alone, Rob turned Jacey to face her. She turned back, but he took her hand, silently insisting she look at him.

"Don't fight me, Katie," he warned. "I fancy my women submissive." His eyes searched her face.

Apparently, Rob expected her to relent. Katie may have. But not Jacey. "I'm not your woman," she whispered crossly. She did not want Lee and Rachel to hear her side of the conversation.

"I stand corrected," he apologized with a wicked grin. "I should have said I expect YE to be submissive."

"What you expect and what you get are two different things!" she hissed.

"I've acquired ye already, and ye well know it," he accused, his blue eyes darkening with anger. "When we were reaching for the tennis ball, ye knew it. If ye would give yourself half a chance now to realize what is happening, ye would not be fighting me at all." His voice seemed remarkably calm in spite of what he was saying to her.

"What are you implying?" she asked, her eyes widening in disbelief. "That I'm easy?"

"What are ye implying?" he answered seductively. "That ye are not?" His blue eyes mocked her question.

"Let me tell you something, Mr. McLennan," she said, her voice raising in volume with her temper. "I don't know where you've received your information, but you've been dead wrong about me from day one!"

"As are all the news articles about your many conquests. Ah, yes, Miss Katie Chester. We get magazines as far away as Galashiels and they print the same disgusting articles for our benefit as for ye Americans. Ye've been on a rebellion campaign since ye were seventeen."

"How dare you!" she slapped his face.

Ignoring her reaction, he mocked, "Surely, ye are not trying to convince me your performance outside with the tennis ball was simple innocence? That ye did not let your eyes linger on my lips for a reason? That ye did not deliberately set out to snare me into some kind of trap, like ye have poor Mr. Carrington?"

"What kind of person do you think I am?" Jacey's voice quivered, realizing that Rob was describing an entirely different individual than herself. Was it her fault she was supposed to act like someone he seemed to despise?

"Think?" he taunted. "Your kind are always in the frying pan, milady. Ye've no need to seek a quick thrill or a ride to the clearing house. Since wealth is no obstacle to ye, this must be your way to get even with your father."

"You're not only conceited and arrogant," she said, her voice shrill. "You're despicable." Jacey raised her hand, intending to slap him once again.

Rob was too quick for her. His hand darted out, catching hers in midair, preventing any contact with his face.

"What's the matter, Miss Katie?" he asked as his grip on her wrist immobilized her. "Does the truth hurt?" he jibed. Then, he flung her hand from his, turned and stalked down the hall and out through the front door.

Jacey remained in the kitchen, her knees quivering, trying to regain her composure. She heard Rob's car roar to life and speed away before Rachel and Lee ventured back to the kitchen.

"Uh-oh," Lee said, calmly observing the torment in Jacey's green eyes. "Trouble with the romance already?"

"There is no romance," Jacey protested hotly. "And you of all people should know it."

"Tell me," he relented, picking up her graceless hint.

"Mr. McLennan is just retaliating," said Jacey.

"It's not like him at all," Rachel offered, her voice echoing around the big kitchen. "He's not one to seek revenge."

"Then he's turning over a new leaf," Jacey sniffed. "And it's not very becoming."

"Let's not let it spoil our day," Lee suggested, putting a broad smile on his face for Jacey's sake, and she knew it. "The three of us can still go on that picnic and have a good day."

Rachel's eyes darted from Jacey to Lee. "Oh, no," she said quickly. "I couldn't go. Not now. I – "

"Please do," Jacey pleaded. "Lee and I would love to have you."

"Yes, we certainly would," Lee agreed.

Although Lee and Rachel did their best to cheer Jacey up the rest of the day, in her heart, it really didn't help. Their picnic was remarkably tame, their conversation polite and informal, with no mention of the irascible Robert Roy McLennan.

Later that night as she curled up in a solitary spoon position upon her bed, a swirling mist brought the heady fragrance of Scottish heather through her open window from the surrounding hills, but Jacey was oblivious of it. She worried, *Why do I want Rob to know the real me, Jacey Munroe, and not just the pampered Katie Chester?*

Chapter Four

On Sunday morning, Jacey refused to stay in bed as long as Katie Chester would have. She hadn't slept all night. Dawn found her staring at the wallpapered ceiling, counting the tiny yellow daisies. Mind exercises like this made her sleepy, but the moment her eyes closed, she recalled Rob's angry expression and heard his taunting words echo in her soul. Her only alternative was to open her eyes and resume counting.

As soon as it was light enough, Jacey dressed in running gear, which Katie Chester apparently thought only came in fuchsia and chartreuse. Jacey slipped quietly out the back door. She had predetermined her running course the day she came down to the stables with Master Forbes. A trail from the stables led westward where she might be afforded some privacy. From maps she had studied on the plane from Washington, D.C., to New York, she knew a lake and a rugged valley stretched before her, largely untouched because of the massive holdings of people like the Forbes and the McLennans.

While Galashiels was a nice-sized little city, it still had its rural areas and its wilderness and sparse woodland where the wealthy lived upon expansive, luxurious estates, giving themselves elbow room few of the middle class would ever know. Forbes Manor was such a place.

Now, Jacey would take advantage of the solitude and spend part of the morning running through the narrow glen.

Jacey stretched and moved her body around, realizing the last few days had taken its toll. She hadn't run since the morning she arrived in Washington, D.C., and was taken straight to Director Stevens' office to learn about this undercover assignment.

Had she foreseen the difficulties she would face with Rob McLennan, she wondered if she would have refused the Director's request. If she had declined the assignment, she may have been terminated. When she signed her contract, her duties were not spelled out in their entirety, and there was always that one non-negotiable clause, "whatever the Government of the United States of America may deem necessary for the greater good of the nation." Jacey had been sworn in under that clause. She knew it, had read it and understood it. But, how much was her country supposed to ask of her? Could she face down Rob McLennan with her heart intact? Jacey had no answer to these questions.

As she began her run, Jacey contemplated her feelings for Rob. She recognized it yesterday on the tennis court, when he thought she was attempting to ensnare him with her womanly guile. But, it was no act for Jacey. His magnetism pulled her in, and she wanted him in ways she'd only dreamed about. Jacey knew it wasn't real love, not yet. However, Jacey feared her feelings could become stronger toward Rob, the longer she was exposed to him. He had some strange, hypnotic force about him that drew Jacey in like a bee to sweet nectar.

Resolved to constantly guard herself against Rob, Jacey realized she would soon find herself trapped between the longings of her heart and the strong will of her mind. She had never been tested previously to see which of the two would rule. It was one challenge she would not enjoy, not when she was striving each day, and moment to moment, to maintain her undercover status.

Running past a recently planted stand of young trees toward the narrow strip of water known as Lake Thistle, Jacey reflected on her life, tucking Rob away for awhile into the deepest recesses of her heart. Her entire existence had been challenging, beginning with the first day her father sent her away to boarding school because he was too busy as a young doctor to give her the attention she needed. Her mother, too, stayed active as an attorney, and Jacey was often left in the summer with lots of time on her hands. She refused to hang out with the rich and powerful youth who were her peers, and threw herself into her studies, graduating high school two years earlier than her classmates. Her university studies failed to challenge her, and she graduated with her bachelor's degree in criminal law by the time she was twenty. She supposed her parents' marriage had been an unhappy one, but she wasn't home long enough with her parents to find out. Then, her mother died suddenly from a brain aneurism that burst, yanking Jacey's safe and secure world out from under her.

After his wife's death, Jacey's father turned to alcohol and drugs. By the time she graduated from the Academy of Aviation at Long Island with her pilot's license, Jacey realized how devastated her father was over his loss, and had legal documents drawn up to protect his interests. She sold the family home and moved with her father to a small condo in the southern part of San Francisco. Desperately, Jacey hoped by getting her father away from New York, away from his old haunting grounds, he would agree to a rehabilitation program. But, he continued to reach out to the unsavory population and was soon back to drinking and drugs. Finally realizing her father could not be helped until he wanted it, she poured herself into her first love, flying, learning how to fly more than a dozen different aircraft. Within a year after moving with her father to San Francisco, Jacey applied for a position with the FBI, was accepted and put through a rigorous training program at Quantico, Virginia, from which she graduated two years later. Since then, Jacey had flown airplanes for the Bureau, transporting agents all around the world. Occasionally, she had been assigned field work, but because she was such an exacting pilot, flying was the normal assignment to which she was called. On her salary, Jacey knew she would never get rich, but she was comfortable.

Although Jacey enjoyed her occupation, she spent her days off looking for unobtrusive ways to insert herself into her father's life, hoping he would eventually realize the valuable time they spent together could never be recaptured. But, living with an alcoholic who was also addicted to drugs was certainly not how she dreamed her life would be when she grew up. She always thought she would be sheltered and treasured as a wife and a mother in a society that cherished womanhood. Career goals had changed, and she had become the primary breadwinner for herself and her dad.

That she was a woman seemed to be against her at every turn in her life, but she'd managed to hurdle every challenge the world had thrown at her, and overcome them all . . . until now. Her reward for perseverance had been both a blessing financially and a mistake emotionally. Now, Jacey regretted accepting the Director's assignment as an undercover agent. *As though I had a choice in the matter.*

Her role as Ms. Katie Chester, rich and beautiful daughter of Lord Myles Chester, was not to be taken lightly. If she failed her mission in Galashiels, it would be her first personal failure. Jacey had fought many battles, but she'd never completely lost any of them.

With each footfall along the damp trail upon which she sped, Jacey reminded herself that she was now – and had always been – a survivor. Her only recourse was to survive whatever trials awaited her, then return to San Francisco to lick her wounds if Rob trampled her heart too severely.

By eleven in the morning, Jacey's run had become the cathartic she needed, allowing her to put off the emotional shackles of Jacey Munroe, and return to Forbes Manor as Katie Chester. She showered and dressed in a hot pink outfit that accented her figure and did nothing to downplay Katie's colorful lifestyle.

Downstairs, Master Forbes was reading the daily paper while Rachel was helping Miriam with a fresh fruit salad in the kitchen.

"When did you take up running?" Rachel asked as she dried her hands on a paper towel. "You always used to sleep late."

"I had a lot of energy to run off," Jacey answered. "Especially after yesterday. Mmm, that salad looks good."

"I promised Rob I would bring his favorite salad with us this evening," Rachel replied. "He's keen on fresh fruits and vegetables. He also prefers whole grains. You'll probably enjoy dinner today."

"I forgot," Jacey lied as she sat down in a wicker chair near the table. "Do you think he'll mind if I skip the dinner invitation? After yesterday, I doubt he wants to face me again."

"That's up to you," Rachel grinned. "But, he did stop by while you were out running this morning. He left you this note." She removed a folded envelope from her apron pocket and handed it to Jacey. "Lee and I were talking on the phone last night, and we've decided Rob must like you."

"Like that would be an empowerment," Jacey said, taking the envelope in what she hoped was a casual manner.

Rachel returned to her salad while Jacey opened the note and read silently to herself:

Dear Miss Katie;

I apologize for my manners of yesterday. Please forgive me by attending dinner at my home this evening at six o'clock.

Affectionately,
Robert Roy McLennan

Jacey closed her eyes for a moment and took a deep breath. It wasn't anything heart-shattering, but he did apologize. She should give him credit for that much. Folding the paper neatly, she returned it to the envelope and tossed it onto the table.

"Are you going?" Rachel asked, noticing Jacey had finished reading.

"I'll think about it." Jacey wasn't about to commit to anything at the moment. Even though Rob had apologized, Jacey intuitively felt that this dinner party was not in her best interest.

She spent three hours grooming Storm with the stableman, getting to know the stallion, feeding him oats and apples, hoping to ride him tomorrow once the horse knew her a little better. Meanwhile, she ignored the thunderclouds hanging over her heart. When she arrived back at Forbes Manor, Rachel and Master Forbes were waiting for her in the parlor.

"You're not going?" asked Rachel. Jacey started to shake her head, but Rachel pleaded, "Oh, you have to, Katie. Lee called to say he's going, as well. He asked me to tell you he'd love to see you there."

In Jacey's mind, coming from Lee it was a direct order and she could not refuse. "Well, if Lee is going," she smiled, hoping her expression exactly matched how Katie Chester would react.

"Good," Rachel giggled. "I chose a gown for you, it's on your bed. And Miriam has drawn a nice warm bath for you."

Jacey shrugged. Keeping herself spaced from Rob McLennan with Rachel around was

not going to be easy. Pensively, she went upstairs and took a long, luxurious bath.

A suitcase had arrived that afternoon. Along
with a few modest evening dresses for Jacey to
wear, she found a pair of charcoal-gray sweat
pants and jacket, a pair of good-quality running
shoes and a light gray tee-shirt. Tucked into a
false bottom of the suitcase, Jacey located her
weapon, a Glock 24. Lee had found a way to
smuggle her gun to her, and Jacey smiled to herself. *Thank you, Lee Carrington.* She put the
sweats in the back of a night stand drawer, along
with her holster and Glock 24, which she rolled
up into the sweat pants. She may not need the
gun, but the occasional threat to FBI agents gave
her pause to be grateful.

Jacey left the dress Rachel had chosen on
the bed, it was entirely too conservative for the
Katie she had been briefed about. Instead, Jacey
slipped into a red silk dress that seemed to whisper, *touch me if you dare*. It was the only dress
Lee had sent that had Katie's mind-set sewn into
the design, but it was far more modest than any
of the skimpy evening gowns Katie had packed
for herself.

Carefully, she tucked the tiny microphone between her cleavage and hoped it would not reveal
the racing of her heart when Rob was near her.

In addition, Jacey wore black patent leather high heels. Since Rob always seemed to tower over her, she hoped the little extra height would help her overcome some of that disadvantage. She should have realized nothing could be advantageous in defending herself against Rob's sharp tongue.

* * * * *

Rob's aunt, MayBelle McLennan, was rounded in all the right places for a woman her age. She had silver, curly hair and dimples deeper than the other wrinkles in her face, as well as sky-blue eyes, a mirror of Rob's own. Otherwise, Jacey saw no resemblance between the two McLennans.

Aunt MayBelle, who insisted everyone call her "Auntie," monopolized the conversation at dinner. Her keen sense of humor kept the party alive. She smiled constantly and patted Rob's hand in a maternal fashion as she told her little stories and adventures.

It seemed apparent that Aunt MayBelle cared deeply for her only nephew, and Jacey was surprised to learn that the noble Rob McLennan had been raised by his aunt. His mother had died in childbirth. His father, devoid of any paternal feeling for the product of his unhappy marriage, left Rob's care and keeping to his sister.

Rob regarded Aunt MayBelle highly, never once correcting her, nor censuring her in any way. Even his eyes seemed to smile when he looked at her.

Lee was unusually quiet through dinner, giving Jacey a furtive glance now and then. Mostly, he smiled at Rachel and seemed to enjoy it when she smiled back at him.

After the meal was finished, they were about to adjourn to the sitting room, when Rob said," Katie has not been given a tour of the house and grounds. Do ye mind?"

His question seemed to be directed at Lee, but Aunt MayBelle answered. "No, love. Not at all. I'm sure I can keep Mr. Carrington and the Forbes company until you return."

Jacey threw Lee a frosty glare. Some friend outside the castle he was, not coming to her rescue. Resigned to her fate, she turned to face Rob.

"I have no doubt of that," Rob said, giving his aunt a kiss on the forehead. Then, he took Jacey by the elbow and escorted her outside into the fragrant and beautiful rose garden.

"Your aunt has such a lovely home," Jacey said, trying to be polite.

"It's mine," he answered, his voice cold and unwelcome. "Come along." Rob took her hand and led her towards a small vegetable garden to the left of a two-story cottage, then past another rose garden and manicured lawns surrounded by tall, ancient sycamore trees. When they were some distance from the house, Rob stopped, released Jacey's hand and turned to face her.

For several silent moments, Rob watched her as she folded her hands behind her back nervously and straightened the pleat in her dress. His shrewd vision did not miss the rise and fall of her chest as she breathed unsteadily under his scrutiny.

Jacey made an attempt to study him, as well, allowing her eyes to stray from his black polished shoes, knee-high stockings and the McLennan tartan kilt he wore with its green, blue, red, black and white plaid. His shoulder cape, known as a fly plaid, was held in place by a five-stoned amethyst brooch with the Scottish Thistle Emblem. Scotland was a part of this man, and his full Scottish outfit testified of his deep roots. To hide her embarrassment over his obvious assessment of her, she imagined him in a tall Stetson, denim jeans and western shirt. He would make a striking cowboy. With the lilt of his accent barely noticeable, his voice would blend in well with western America.

He broke the reverence of her gaze with harsh words. "I cannot bring myself to trust ye, Katie Chester."

Her eyes flew to his as he bored into her soul painfully.

"Why?" she asked patiently. "Whatever have I done to earn your distrust?" She was not about to let him see how much he intimidated her, nor how much his words scalded.

"Ye are always pretending," he answered.

She had to appreciate his honesty, if nothing else.

Rob continued, "Though why a woman of your standing in the world would feel it necessary to put on an act, I cannot understand. It seems that ye are hiding something. I cannot put my finger on it yet." He paused. "But, I will."

Standing with his shoulders squared, his back straight, his head tilted just enough to let her search his silver-blue eyes in the moonlight for several intense moments, he glared into her heart.

Jacey strived for control of the situation, refusing to allow his emotional intrusion. Gathering courage, she asked, "Because my eyes lingered on your lips yesterday, you accuse me. Was that a crime?"

He wrapped strong hands around her arms, pulling her against him. "I wish that were all," he said, his voice husky, almost panicked. "Ye do not know how badly I wish that were all."

He gave her no time to react before his lips were upon hers, tasting and lingering. She trembled in his arms. To her amazement, she responded to his kiss by placing her hands behind his neck, her fingers curled in his thick auburn hair. For a moment, time came to a glorious, reverent standstill, waiting for them to finish. Deep within her a longing to let his embrace go on forever overwhelmed her. Desire leapt through her veins and she let him pull her closer.

Just as abruptly as his kiss began, Rob pushed her away from him, wiping his mouth with his hand. "Ye act like a woman of means on rare occasions," he challenged. "Other times, ye seem too real, too tender to have been raised in luxury. 'Tis almost as if ye are a complete and separate entity from whom ye claim."

Eyes widening, Jacey put her hand over her mouth to prevent herself from gasping. Her thoughts worked overtime, and she responded in haste, her role as Katie Chester firmly planted in her mind. "You speak of trust," she said, her voice dripping in disgust. "But trust is earned, and you are a man . . . with a criminal record. You've no right to speak to me of trust."

Immediately, Jacey regretted what she'd said. How could she explain how she knew? Why had she revealed something Lee had discovered in Rob's background? Jacey wanted nothing more than to flee. She spun around, hoping to distance herself from him.

Just as quickly, he grabbed her arms and pulled her backwards, wrapping his strong arms around her waist. Of course, she knew how to get out of such an embrace, but even her strong will could not force her to do it. To her great dismay, she learned that her heart could win over a battle with her mind.

Consequently, Jacey took the only reaction available. She relaxed against him, letting him hold her, enjoying the moment, wishing his actions were not controlled by his anger.

Finally, he explained, "I was only nineteen when it happened. How did ye know?"

"I have my sources," she admitted, faking her words as she went along. "As you know, with wealth comes wariness. I've had a background service provider for years. You thought I wouldn't check you out the moment you showed an ounce of interest?"

"Drunk and disorderly at nineteen, Katie. I was still a very young man, and it was a one-time offense. I suppose ye have also learned I've been a teetotaler ever since?" His voice sounded ragged, hurt somehow.

"I have," Jacey admitted.

"That was my last mistake, Katie," he pleaded.

"In your opinion." She almost laughed. "You've a terrible temper, Robert Roy McLennan. And it's going to be your downfall."

"Brave predictions from a woman who sails through life on pretense," he barked, pushing her roughly away from him. "Ye've made your prediction. Now, I'll make mine. When I sort through the pieces of your life and discover what ye are trying so desperately to hide, I'll come looking for ye. It's a day ye should not look forward to, Miss Katie Chester."

Jacey did not turn around to face him. She held her head proudly and walked back to the house, knowing his eyes were upon her the entire way.

Chapter Five

Rob McLennan paced back and forth outside Lee Carrington's hotel room door, debating if he should stay the course. Sickened by how he felt, by what he must do to obtain any semblance of peace in his mind regarding Katie Chester, Rob agonized over his decision to visit Lee Carrington. He planned to extract whatever information he could from the man.

Somehow, he would have to learn to trust Katie Chester, either that or – the alternative was too terrible to consider. *But, like this?* he asked himself. *Should I pursue knowledge of Katie by risking the destruction of her friendship with Lee Carrington?* Finally shaking his head, Rob turned to walk away.

A telephone rang within Lee's hotel room. Rob cringed as he heard Lee answer it. Amazingly, the door seemed to amplify sound within the room, and Rob pressed his ear quietly against it, eavesdropping.

"Carrington here," were Lee's first uttered words.

Rob listened quietly, but for several seconds, Lee said nothing. Then, Lee soothed, "Calm down, J.C., calm down." A brief pause, "We can deal with this. Let me reassure you."

Waiting, Rob wondered who this J.C. was, and what he was upset about. Then, "We're on top of it, J.C. Yes, Rob McLennan could ruin the entire mission. But, I have no intention of letting him."

After another pause, Lee said, " They're still uncertain Ms. Chester is out of danger. Yes, he is interfering in procuring her safety."

Concerns swept into Rob's heart. It seemed obvious that Lee was working with someone else in an orchestrated effort to keep Katie safe. It left no doubt in Rob's mind who was interfering. Rob had unwittingly become the interloper in an obvious American operation. Somehow, Rob would have to take drastic measures to eliminate Lee's doubts concerning him.

Pressing his ear once more to the door, Rob heard the last few words of Lee's conversation.

" . . . after midnight tomorrow. Very well. Carry on, J.C. We'll talk more then."

Silently, Rob slipped away from the hotel, hoping no one had noticed his presence. Retreating to McLennan Hall, he paced the floors of his ancestral home until dawn, unable to sleep, unable to decide on a course of action.

He returned to the hotel early the next morning, where he found Lee Carrington in the breakfast room. As soon as Lee had ordered, Rob sat down opposite him.

"Good morning, Rob, may I persuade you to join me?" quipped Lee.

"Sorry for the intrusion, but I need to speak with ye about young Katie," said Rob.

Lee's interest was captured, but Rob began to notice how keenly Lee surveyed their surroundings, keeping his attention on Rob while covertly exploring the faces and posturing of people within the small restaurant, probably to determine if they posed any danger. It surprised Rob that he had not noticed Lee's behavior before now, for he had seen the exact same peculiar mannerisms in Lee the day Katie was kissing Lee all over his face. Several times, Rob had noticed Katie doing the same thing. This knowledge almost unnerved him, but he chose to continue his conversation with Lee, regardless.

"I came alone, Lee, and no one knows I am here, I assure ye," began Rob.

"About Katie," said Lee, directing Rob back to his original topic.

"How serious are your intentions concerning her?" asked Rob.

The waiter arrived, so Rob gave his order, then when the waiter left, Lee said, "My intentions should not concern you, Rob. I think we're both mature enough to put our feelings aside for Katie and keep our focus on her safety."

"You mean to say she is in danger?" asked Rob.

Lee slipped three photographs from inside a jacket pocket and slid them toward Rob. They were time stamped, showing Rob in a pacing mode outside Lee's hotel room, listening at the door, and leaving the hotel floor. To his dismay, Rob learned his actions last night had been discovered.

"How much of my conversation did you hear last night?" Lee asked. "Before you answer, may I remind you the U.S. Government still has some political clout in Scotland. One call to the Yard and your entire estate and business properties could be seized, and your aunt could be detained. Right now, I would like nothing more than to incarcerate you until you no longer pose a threat to Katie Chester."

"Who does Katie need protection from?" Rob asked.

"Besides yourself?" Lee countered.

"I would never harm Katie," Rob insisted.

"No, you just want to scare her to death . . . or tear her heart in small pieces and toss them out over the glen on a windy day." Lee's eyes narrowed. His expression became increasingly grim.

"I admit, I have had difficulty trusting the lass," Rob confessed after considering that complete honesty may be the best policy at the moment. "She acts oddly from her true self, and I find her manner unconvincing."

"She's fragile," admitted Lee. "Someone intends to harm her, and she's worried you might be working for him."

"Me? I have no reason to work for this unsavory character ye describe. I am an employer, not an employee. Surely ye know this, ye've no doubt investigated me thoroughly by now."

"We have," said Lee, "and we scrutinize wealthy men, and the secrets they hide, more closely than any others."

"I have nothing to hide," Rob offered. "The only thing amiss in my life occurred over ten years ago, but then I'm sure ye know I was arrested when I was nineteen. I'm equally certain ye are the one who told Miss Katie about my record. She knows who ye are, and why ye are here, doesn't she?"

"Now, see, that's the interesting thing," Lee mused aloud. "In my line of work, I ask the questions and people like you answer them. It's not the other way around."

"Ask me whatever ye wish," insisted Rob.

Lee smiled. "Very well. What are your intentions regarding Katie Chester?"

Rob worried how to answer. He had feelings, but he also had distrust. Finally, he said, "I am intrigued by her and I want to understand her better. Until that happens, I'm afraid I can have no intentions of any kind toward her."

"What will it take for you to lower your guard and stop scaring the poor girl?" Lee asked, though Rob could tell it was more demand than question.

"Trust comes to mind."

"Trust is earned, Rob. It is not granted automatically, nor out of fear. I reminded Katie of this fact the moment I spoke with her after your eavesdropping at my door last night. Surely, you see the reasons why she does not trust you."

Surprised at Lee's response, Rob mused aloud, "I thought it was the other way around."

Shaking his head, Lee remained quiet as their breakfast arrived, then both men began devouring their food wholeheartedly.

As they ate, Rob wondered when Lee would continue questioning him, and was surprised when Lee finally suggested, "It would make things easier for everyone if you would call a truce between yourself and Ms. Chester. Expect nothing more or less from Katie than who she is, and put away your concerns regarding her."

"May I ask a question in return for my complete cooperation?"

"You may ask," Lee warned. "I cannot guarantee I will answer."

"Who is this J.C. ye were speaking with last night?"

When Lee seemed to pale visibly, Rob asked quickly, " Is he perhaps another agent working closer to the hub of Katie's safety wheel?"

"Agent J.C. Munroe," Lee answered, emphasizing the *agent*.

"Ye *are* FBI, then?" Rob asked. "And, Agent J.C. Munroe?"

"Sorry, Rob. If I told you who *he* is – "

Rob nodded, gave a wry smile and interrupted with, "– ye'd have to kill me, right?"

"Something like that," agreed Lee.

"Am I permitted to continue seeing Miss Katie? Or, now that I am privy to certain secrets, must I keep my distance?" asked Rob, wondering how far he dare push Lee before the man's patience waned.

"She is not a commodity for which we trade secrets for visitations, Rob. You are friends with the Forbes. I expect your absence would probably upset all of them, including Katie. Simply be aware that she is never out of our sight. If you are within a hundred-yard radius of her, you are in our line of fire, and I mean that literally."

Shocked by this confession, Rob pushed. "If ye have weapons trained upon her, perhaps I should stand in close proximity of Katie at all times and insist we both wear body armor."

"Katie will never be in the crosshairs of the U.S. Government, Rob. It is yourself with whom you should be concerned. You came this close last night to feeling the wrath of the triggerman's finger," Lee said, putting his thumb and forefinger almost together.

"I see," said Rob. "I will restrain my temper in future encounters."

"As Katie warned you last night, that would be wise, even if our agents were not in the picture," suggested Lee.

Rob could understand the concern for keeping Katie safe from himself. Had he known she was under such heavy guard, he would have understood a little more why the lass continued to puzzle him. However, he came away from breakfast wondering why the FBI considered it necessary to provide protection for Katie at all. Who would want to hurt her? And why? Those two questions, Lee never answered.

Lee had told Rob just enough to keep him on his guard, but more than enough for him to feel Katie could be in real danger. Rob had also seen too many movies and television programs, downplaying the ability of the U.S. government to protect anyone from someone who truly intended to harm them. Rob resolved his temper would have to be shelved, since he intended to stay closer to Katie than ever before. If the FBI failed to protect Katie for whatever reasons, perhaps he could succeed.

* * * * *

Jacey awakened to a songbird's pleasant melody outside her bedroom window. It gave her a tremendous boost of morale to awaken in the countryside. She had never known such freedom from smog, noise and fast-paced living before now. Fond memories such as these would always hold a treasured place within her heart.

For a moment, Jacey worried about Rob. She knew Lee intended to see him this morning, after telephoning her about Rob's eavesdropping event last night. In fact, Jacey had stayed awake several hours worrying about how their conversation would turn out, and what Rob had overheard. Finally, sleep had found her . . . sweet and peaceful sleep.

She rolled over in bed, wondering what time it was and why the house was still so quiet. To her alarm, Rob stood in the doorframe, a breakfast tray in his hand like a waiter in a luxury hotel.

"Good morning, lass," he said, giving her a bright smile. "Everyone else has eaten. Rachel persuaded Lee to take her shopping this morning, and Master Forbes has already left for work. Miriam gave me permission to bring you breakfast."

"You're not going to throw it at me, are you?" she asked, as she pulled the blanket up to her chin.

Rob laughed aloud, and Jacey wondered if she had awakened in some sort of dream, caught between reality and fantasy. To keep the dream going, she teased, "You don't plan on force-feeding me?"

More laughter.

Jacey slowly sat up in bed. "I'm warning you, I'm like a cat with nine lives. If you throw me out the window, I'll only land feet first."

"I thought we should call a truce," Rob said, bringing the breakfast tray to her and placing it over her lap.

"What for?" she teased. "I thought we got along splendidly."

"Miss Katie Chester," Rob said, bowing gracefully. "I apologize for errors I have made in the past, and I ask that you forgive me. In return, I will do my best to keep my temper under control."

"Like that will ever happen," she said, looking at the eggs, bacon and Scottish oatcakes on the tray, accompanied by a single yellow rose, which Jacey picked up and smelled. "Mmm. A very nice touch," she said. "Your idea, I suppose."

Rob nodded, grinning.

"All right, who are you?" she asked. "And what have you done with that ogre, Master McLennan?"

"Ogre?" he questioned. "I'm wounded, Katie. Ogre?"

"Well," she relented. "Not this morning . . . yet."

"Ye had to qualify that, didn't ye?"

"Absolutely."

"The truth is, I've had a little talk with your friend, Lee Carrington. He assures me that my fears concerning ye are unwarranted."

"I don't know what Lee persuaded you to believe, but I'm still just as ill-tempered as always, and if you think you can trust me now, you are sadly mistaken."

"An interesting thing, trust. It is earned, or so you told me last evening, and Lee reminded me this morning."

Jacey didn't know quite how to take this new version of Rob McLennan. "And, I haven't earned your trust yet, so why are you now pretending that I have?"

"Something Lee said helped that, I believe," Rob explained.

"Really? And what was that?" she asked.

"He suggested that perhaps the reason why I was having difficulty trusting ye, was simply because ye do not trust me. I felt it an interesting, almost analogous thought between us, that perhaps the two of us are more alike than I had earlier considered. Ye cannot relax and be yourself around me, because ye do not trust me. It was the same for me. One of us must break this cycle, and I am the man, it is up to me to do the right thing."

"Like women can't do the right thing, merely because they are women?" she asked, sensing a tautness to her voice.

"Women are the gentler sex, that is what I meant. It is up to us men to lead the way for ye."

Now, Jacey laughed. "You've just set civilization back two hundred years, Rob. One day I'll show you how tough we women can really be."

"I look forward to the day," smiled Rob. "But, I do see an argument forming in your mind, so I will let ye eat your breakfast in peace. Rachel tells me ye like to run in the morning. If I may have your permission, I would like to run with ye."

"Good plan," said Jacey. "We'll see who's the gentler sex then, won't we?"

Rob did not respond, but stepped from the room and closed the door.

Relieved, Jacey ate an oatcake, drank her milk and juice, and left the rest for Master Forbes' dogs. After pulling on some running clothes, vivid fuchsia once again, *I swear Katie Chester doesn't know other colors exist!* she sprayed her hair with water and finger-combed through her coiled locks, watching in amazement as each red curl sprang back into its disarrayed place.

Within minutes, Jacey and Rob were running along the trail that led through the glen and past the Forbes' private lake. While they ran, Jacey noticed a stream that meandered up the dale, and wondered if she followed it to the top sometime when she was riding Storm, how far she could see from the summit.

Halfway through their run, they stopped long enough to get a drink of water from the plastic bottles strapped to their waists. Rob was winded, and Jacey gave him a little extra time to recover.

"Have you been swimming in the lake?" Jacey asked while she waited for Rob to cool down.

"Aye, and 'tis cold, Katie. It takes a stout heart to swim in these lochs, lass."

"Should I take that as a personal challenge?" she wondered aloud.

"No, I wouldn't challenge ye to something like that. 'Twould take your breath away to jump in, and many a soul has lost their lives in lochs like this one."

"Are you ready to start back?" Jacey asked.

She almost saw a grimace cross his face, but he erased it and smiled steadily. "As soon as ye are, Miss Katie."

"Let's go, then," she said, taking the lead.

By the time they reached Forbes Manor, Rob was so winded he had to lay down upon the grass and rest. "I can see ye are in much better condition than I, lass," he admitted.

"Give yourself two weeks of running like that every morning, and you'll be amazed at how much better you'd manage it."

"We must have run ten miles," he complained.

"Four," she argued. "At home, I keep a pedometer, and I can tell how far it is without clocking myself, anymore."

"Well, then it feels like ten miles," Rob confessed. "Perhaps I owe ye an apology, accusing ye of being the weaker sex."

"If you apologize once more today," Jacey warned, "I'll know you're not the real Rob McLennan, but a clone sent to confuse me."

It was good to have a reprieve from Rob's anger, although Jacey couldn't help wondering when it would return. She also worried about her feelings toward Rob. It was easier to dislike him when he was ornery. This nice side scared her far more than his angry side. It opened her heart up to emotions that made her more vulnerable, feelings she was less able to ignore or control.

Chapter Six

Every morning for the next few weeks, Rob showed up bright and early to run with Jacey. Lee and Rachel had taken to running with them, as well, and they often brought picnic supplies in backpacks, enjoying the fresh air and the countryside more than Jacey ever thought she could. She learned to love the green rolling hills of Scotland's borders, and dreaded returning to the smog, heat and noise of San Francisco.

Staying to his proposed truce, Rob became a true gentleman, always considerate of Jacey's needs, always nearby, but never allowing himself to get too close. Respecting this decision on his part, Jacey made no attempt to "lure him in," as he had accused her on her first week at Forbes Manor. They became friends, and for now that was enough.

This distancing gave Jacey time to get to know Rob, and to care about him in ways she hadn't expected. She wasn't ready to concede she was in love with him, but she couldn't deny the many ways he had of disturbing her emotions when she least expected it. Sometimes, all it took was a simple glance, or the brushing of their hands together as they reached for something from the picnic basket at the same time. On the numerous day trips they took into the city, while sitting beside him in the car, his thigh inches from hers, Jacey was keenly aware of their nearness, and often found herself aflame with desire. Watching the wind ripple his hair, or the dimples in his cheeks when he smiled, sent her emotions tumbling around inside her heart.

When her first month at Forbes Manor ended, Jacey knew their friendship was too good to remain on neutral territory much longer. The more time they spent together, the more she wanted him to stay.

One afternoon, Rob rode his horse, Shadow, over to Forbes Manor. They planned to ride horses up to the top of the glen for a picnic. Weather reports for mid-July called for sun and more sun, and Jacey was glad when Lee and Rachel preferred to stay behind and play a game of tennis.

Expecting to return to Forbes Manor before nightfall, Rob and Jacey coaxed Shadow and Storm up along the stream she had wanted to climb a month ago. The trek was arduous, and many times they had to urge the horses onward with commanding force. But, it was certainly worth the effort when they reached the summit, for they could see the towering old buildings of Galashiels way off in the distance, along with several of the roads and highways.

"Look to the south, Katie, for 'tis England ye see in yon distance." Rob pointed. "And to the east is Galashiels proper."

"I expected more forests," Jacey admitted. "But, the heather is beautiful. I never imagined heather came in so many colors, but here are yellows, pinks and purples of all shades. And, the Scottish thistle is everywhere."

"Legend gives thistle its place in history," Rob explained. "The prickly, thistle saved Scotland back in the thirteenth century when a Norwegian army invaded under cover of darkness. Removing their shoes, hoping to sneak upon the clansmen unaware, one of the unfortunate Norwegians stumbled upon a thistle, screamed out in pain, and awakened the Scotsmen to the invasion. Needless to say, the Scots won that battle."

"Were there trees here in the thirteenth century?" Jacey asked.

"Certainly, lass," said Rob, dismounting and wrapping the reins from the harness around a large boulder. "But, Scotland's government has already begun a reforesting project that will return a good share of our forests to us."

Jacey stood up in the stirrups, then gracefully swung herself out of the saddle. She secured Storm a short distance from Shadow so each could munch on the soft grasses mixed in amongst all the moss, thistle and wild heather.

Rob spread a blanket out and opened up a picnic basket where fruits, cheeses and fresh breads became a tasty picnic, along with Miriam's specialty, home-canned peach juice.

All afternoon, Rob pointed out little hamlets and points of interest in the border areas in Scotland, using binoculars to show her the pinnacle at Galashiels Academy, several of the other stately manor houses off in the distance, as well as small streams and creeks that flowed down into the River Tweed that ran through the town of Galashiels.

He brought his bagpipes, which he played beautifully, and he taught her to sing the famous ballad, *The End of the Road*, by Sir Harry Lauder.

Jacey especially loved the ending, and found herself humming it in her heart the rest of the day:

> "Tho' you're tired and weary, still journey on,
> Till you come to your happy abode,
> Where all the love you've been dreaming of,
> ***Will be there at the end of the road.***"

By early evening, they were laying side by side on the blanket, watching cloud formations and trying to decide what shapes they took. Rob lifted himself up on one elbow and studied Jacey's face as she described what looked like a big fat frog in the sky.

"Ye are a beautiful woman, Katie," he murmured when a lull in the conversation stretched between them. "Why is it that ye color your hair red, when 'tis clearly a golden shade of brown?"

"All women color their hair," she said, ignoring his comment as best she could.

"Ye wear contact lenses, too," Rob observed. "But, what is the real color of your eyes, Lass?"

To this remark, Jacey rolled away from him. "If you notice my contacts, you're definitely too close," she complained, sitting up and pulling her knees up to her chest. She wrapped her arms around them while resting her head upon them, her face away from Rob.

"I don't mean to offend ye, Katie. But, a beautiful woman like yourself should have no need for all the artificial equipment." He reached out and put his fingers into her thick, curly locks.

If only Jacey could tell Rob the truth about herself, but as Lee pointed out several times, the only way to protect the real Katie Chester was to continue the charade. As long as Myles Chester thought his daughter was still staying at Forbes Manor, the FBI stood a chance of keeping Katie safe. Recently, Ms. Chester had been moved to another safe-house because the last one had been accidentally compromised. In the meantime, Jacey had no choice but to fulfill her assignment.

"I like to experiment with different looks," she explained. "When I feel comfortable with my own appearance, then I'll stop. Until then, you'll have to get used to the way I am now."

"'Tis the problem we face, isn't it? Ye seem unwilling to share whom ye are now. We've spent all this time together, and I've not heard ye mention one thing about your life before ye arrived at Forbes Manor. It's as though ye have no past, other than the news articles and magazine interviews I've read. Who is Katie Chester?

'Tis what I'd like to understand most. How can ye be so warm and tender and fun to be with, yet so unwilling to share with me how ye came to this point in your life?"

"I thought Lee told you all you needed to know," she whispered, afraid to look back at him, for fear that even her contact lenses could not hide the feelings she had developed for Rob McLennan.

"Why do ye need protection from someone, Katie? Who is it that's trying to harm ye?" he asked, his voice a ragged blend of frustration and concern.

"The less you know, the safer I am. I cannot tell you more than that, Rob. Please don't ask me again."

"'Tis killing me slowly," he confessed, "wondering each moment, are ye safe? Who's watching over ye today, Katie? I've not seen any evidence of your FBI agents behind any hills or rocks today. 'Tis a difficult place to hide up here at the summit. Down by the lake, I don't doubt there are people watching over ye. But up here? Where's your Agent Munroe, at least?"

Jacey couldn't help but smile. Rob was trying so hard to understand, yet she could tell him nothing. "Oh, J.C.'s around, have no fear of that. Besides, J.C. Munroe is one of the best agents I know."

"Let's say 'twas I ye should fear," he suggested. "'Twas I from whom ye have been hiding in Galashiels."

"Don't tell me that," she said. "I'd have to call in the troops."

"What troops?" he insisted. "There's no one here, but ye and me."

Jacey pulled herself up into a standing position and looked down at Rob. Surely, he wasn't suggesting that he really was part of Myles Chester's elaborate plot to keep her away from the Department of Justice in Washington D.C. *He couldn't be.* Yet, a part of her believed it could be true. Rob was wealthy, and the rich have a tendency to stick together, don't they?

Rob stood up and faced her, reaching out to stroke her cheek. Jacey pulled away from him. "Don't touch me," she warned.

"Katie, what is going through that beautiful head of yours? Ye surely don't believe I could have anything to do with whoever wants to hurt ye?" he asked.

"You put those thoughts in my head, Rob. Why? Are you in on the plot? Tell me!" she demanded.

"No, Katie, I am not," he denied. "I want to protect ye. Why do ye think I've spent the past month by your side, nearly every step of the way?

I don't trust the FBI to protect ye. Nor do I trust Lee Carrington to protect ye. Where is Lee today? Off romancing Rachel. Where is Agent Munroe? He's nowhere to be seen. I know not what other agents ye may have at your beck and call, but I see no evidence they are near. What protection would ye have if it were me ye needed to worry about?"

As if to answer his question, a helicopter with big, almost silent propellers swooped up over the nearest hill and headed straight for them. Jacey recognized it immediately, but Rob panicked. He grabbed her hand as though to take her on a race away from the chopper.

Jacey pulled back on his hand so hard, Rob fell backward onto his buttocks, tearing his pants in the process. She couldn't help laughing at him.

The pilot tipped his hat to her and she waved the helicopter on, shouting, "I'm fine. He's harmless."

Then, she helped Rob to his feet as he rubbed his sore rear and tried to keep his exposure to a minimum.

"Does that answer your question?" she asked. "I'm wired for sound, Rob. Everything you say to me goes back to them. You have only yourself to blame for this. Come on, we need to get back now."

"Everything?" he asked, wincing as he swung up into the saddle.

"Everything," she insisted, gracefully mounting Storm.

"They knew ye kissed Lee Carrington that day in the kitchen?" Rob asked.

"Yes." Jacey made a clicking sound with her tongue and put a little pressure against Storm's flank with her heels. The magnificent animal started ambling a zig-zag course down the hill, Rob and Shadow following closely behind.

"Why would ye do that on tape to one of their agents?" Rob asked, coming alongside her.

"I don't know," she admitted. "Rebellion, I suppose. And the thrill of the chase. I kissed you, too. It's all logged in at their command post."

"All of it?"

"Every word, every whisper, every kiss."

"Then, nothing between us has ever been private."

"Not hardly." She shook her curls.

"Ye make it very difficult for a man to court ye, Katie Chester."

Jacey shrugged. "It's supposed to be this way, Rob. Surely you know that once the threat is over, we'll say goodbye and I'll go back home."

"I had not thought that far ahead," he admitted. He remained silent the rest of the journey down the hill.

He's fuming again, Jacey worried. What could she do to cheer him up?

It was nearly dark when they reached the bottom of the dale, and headed their horses along the lake trail toward Forbes Manor. "Race you to the dock," suggested Jacey, knowing how much Rob liked a challenge.

"You're on!" he said, jabbing Shadow with his stirrups. "Go!"

"Hyah!" Jacey yelled, she and Storm following quickly.

Suddenly, Shadow tripped on a rock in the trail and rolled over forwards, Rob sailing over the horse's head and right in front of him as Shadow whinnied and landed on Rob's foot. Rob scrambled to get out of the way, but he was too late.

Then, Storm, coming up so closely behind them, tried to jump over Shadow and Rob, but his right rear hoof caught Shadow's reins on the way. A sickening crunch sounded when Storm's ankle hit the ground first, and Jacey went flying out of the saddle, through the air and landing on her chest in front of Rob and the horses.

Instinct kicked in immediately. Jacey jumped up, disregarding any damage to herself, and hurried back to Rob, who was trying to stand on his injured foot, but couldn't manage it without agonizing pain. "Hold still," she insisted. "Sit down."

Rob followed her request, and waited while she slipped off his boot to check for breaks. Pulling his stocking off, her fingers deftly felt the bones and tendons, asking where it hurt worse, a technique her father had taught her well. When she was finally satisfied that his foot was not broken, just misaligned, she gave him her riding glove and said, "Here, bite on this."

"Why, what are ye planning to do?"

When he least expected it, Jacey yanked his foot forward and down, realigning it quickly. "I said bite on it," Jacey complained.

"Ow! What did ye do to me?" he growled.

"Move it around," she answered.

Rob gingerly flexed his ankle. Then, realizing that she had indeed repaired it, he said, "Thanks. That does feel a mite better."

"It's not broken," she said. "But, it will be sore. Now, help me with the horses. I think Storm broke his right rear leg, just above the ankle, and Shadow's probably got torn ligaments in his front shoulder."

Rob and Jacey worked with Storm first, calming him down, removing the saddle and splinting the horse's hind right ankle with pipes from Rob's bagpipe, and Rob's belt, to alleviate some of Storm's pain. They also removed Shadow's saddle to keep him comfortable.

"Why aren't your people here yet?" Rob asked when Jacey and he finally sat down beside the two resting horses and stroked them to keep them calm.

"Don't know," said Jacey. "Let me look." She turned away from him, lifted her shirt and pulled a small metallic disk-shaped piece of electronics from inside a small cotton envelope sewn into her bra. "It's broken," she said, pulling her shirt back down and placing the twisted disk in the palm of his hand. Turning back to Rob, she explained, "It must have broken when I landed face first in the dirt."

"Aye, and we should have taken care of your injuries, as well," Rob moaned. "Look at ye."

"That's a little difficult right now," she said, "since I haven't got a mirror."

"Wait here," he said, turning to one of the saddle bags. He removed a bottle of water and a table napkin, and used them to wipe away the dirt and smudges on Jacey's face. By this time, the moon had risen up over the hill and it shone upon them brilliantly. "Hmm," he said huskily. "It looks like your eyes are a golden brown. Almost the color of your hair."

Instinctively, Jacey put her hands up to her face. "I've lost a contact lens," she moaned.

Rob removed her hands gently. "Don't," he persuaded. "I like the color of your eyes. Will ye remove the other one?"

"No, Rob." Jacey hurried over to Storm's saddle and removed a contact case from inside the emergency kit she carried with her everywhere. Quickly, she inserted another contact into her eye and felt to make sure the other contact was still in place.

"Ye carry spares?" he asked, apparently surprised.

"When you're half-blind without them, you have no choice," Jacey answered.

"But, ye set my foot and took care of the animals, all without your one lens," he reminded.

"Adrenalin," she explained, sitting back beside Storm and stroking his neck.

Rob nodded, but he did not comment. After a few moments, he sat beside her and asked, "How long before your people realize ye are not transmitting and find us?"

"I don't know," she said. "It's dark now, but they'll have my point of impact, so it shouldn't take too long."

"That means, until they get here, they won't hear our conversation?"

Jacey froze momentarily. What did Rob have in mind? Finally, she answered, "No, I suppose they won't."

He smiled, then stroked her unmarred cheek with the curl of his fingers. "Which means, we might have a few minutes of privacy, Katie."

Just hearing Katie's name, and not her own, made Jacey cringe. She knew he was going to kiss her, and she wanted him to kiss her desperately. At the same time, she kept hearing Katie's name, remembering Rob thought she was Katie Chester.

Regardless of the tumultuous emotions she felt, Jacey found herself eager the moment his lips touched hers, wishing with all her heart that the rescue crew would not show up for a long, long time. It only took a few kisses to fire a flame within her so strong she trembled. For the first time in her life, Jacey wanted to be loved, wanted to–

When Rob removed his lips from hers, he whispered, "What ye do to me, Katie. I cannot begin to tell ye."

Hearing Katie's name again was exactly what Jacey needed to stop him. "No, Rob. We can't." She pushed against his chest until he re-

leased her, an expression of confusion and surprise on his face. Jacey turned away from him,
tears threatening to spill from her eyes.

"What is it, Katie?" he asked, apparently
bewildered.

Jacey voiced the only response she was allowed to give him. "You know I have to go back
to my father when this is over."

"Ye are worried what your father will think
of me?" Rob questioned.

"It's more complicated than that," she said,
blinking back her tears. Jacey stood up. "I see
lights on the road ahead. Someone's bringing
the Landrover for us."

Chapter Seven

"It was an accident," Jacey said for the third time, listening for anyone to speak to her through the satellite phone she held to her ear. "We shouldn't have been racing when it was already getting dark, but we were. It's not Rob's fault. I'm the one who challenged him to a race."

"He should have known better than to accept," Lee scolded. He was sitting in her bedroom at the vanity, soldering the electronic microphone she had been wearing earlier that night. "Besides, what was the problem up on top of the hill today?"

"He doesn't think the Bureau is watching over me closely enough," she admitted. "I guess he's taken it upon himself to protect me."

"He is one crazy Scot!" Lee grumbled. "He thinks he can outmaneuver the FBI?"

"I – I think he's falling for me," she admitted, letting the tears well up in her eyes and trickle down her cheeks.

Lee looked up at her from the vanity. "I was worried about that. What is it with Scottish romances?" he asked. "I am totally gone on Rachel."

"Really?" asked Jacey, eager to trade topics of conversation.

Nodding, Lee said, "I can't tell her who I am because it will give away your cover, but I'm afraid I'll lose her when she learns the truth some other way."

"Lee," she reminded, using her best conspiratorial voice. "We're supposed to be professionals. We don't let our feelings get in the way of our assignments."

"Yes, I know. I just said those words to you." He soldered a piece of metal onto the disk to mend one of the hair-thin connections. When it cooled, he said, "Testing, one two – "

"I've got it," came a voice on Jacey's satellite phone.

"They've got it," she repeated.

"Okay," Lee sighed in approval. "Put this back on, and no more horses."

"Easy for you to say. It's my fault they're both hurt. Storm's still with the vet, but at least Shadow is going to be okay."

Lee stood up and handed her the disk. "Are you in love with Rob?"

"I can't be," she denied. "He's falling for Katie Chester, and that's not – "

Lee quickly put a hand over her mouth. "Shh. You know how he likes to listen behind closed doors."

Jacey removed his hand and went to the bedroom door, opened it and stepped onto the landing. From her position, she could see Rob was still on the telephone downstairs in the parlor. His leg was propped up on a pillow and a bag of ice surrounded his ankle. Returning to her bedroom and closing the door, she complained softly to Lee, "He's falling for someone who's not me," she insisted.

Lee argued, "He's falling for you, he just doesn't know who you are."

Jacey nodded. "Espionage is more difficult than I imagined. Now, I know why I wanted to be a pilot for the Bureau and not a field officer."

"Do you love him?" Lee asked a second time.

"I don't know," she admitted. "Sometimes I think I do. Other times, I convince myself I don't. Especially when he calls me Katie, I – "

"It's part of the burden we carry," Lee consoled. "No one ever said undercover work was easy, but it's a vital part of what we do."

"How much longer must we dance through this charade?" Jacey asked, aching with emotional pain more intense than any scrapes or bruises she'd received.

"Hopefully," he grinned, "before your face heals up."

Jacey slipped into the bathroom and looked at her face in the mirror. Her left cheek and forehead had road rash, but fortunately, she'd been able to tweeze all the little pieces of dirt out of it. A good coating of antibiotic ointment made her face shine back at her.

"Is there anything else I can do for you tonight?" Lee asked.

"Yes, there is. But, only if Rachel is still down in the stables."

"What?"

"I want you to kiss me goodnight, with Rob watching."

"That's rather drastic. Are you sure you want to put him off you that far?"

"It's the only way to maintain my cover," she admitted. "If I hadn't seen the Landrover's lights tonight, I was going to turn back around and tell him the truth. This way, he'll get angry, and we won't talk to one another for a week or two."

"If you're sure that's what you want," Lee agreed.

"Only if Rachel's not around, though," insisted Jacey. "I don't want to rock your boat."

"Why don't I go first?" suggested Lee. "You follow me in a rush, and we'll take it from there." He rubbed her shoulder and turned to leave.

"Thanks, Lee. I think it's the only way." Jacey swallowed a lump in her throat. She glanced out the window toward the stables. The lights were still on, and there was no indication that anyone was coming up to the manor house. "The coast is clear," she said.

Lee left the bedroom and Jacey waited with the door slightly ajar until he was near the bottom step. Rob was no longer on the telephone, but he was watching Lee descend. Forcing herself to move, Jacey opened the door and said, hesitantly at first, "Lee?"

He turned to face her. "What is it, Katie?"

Tears streamed down her cheeks. This would be the finest performance of her life, but she felt that she had no choice. Her tears were not for Lee, and they both knew it. Rob, however, did not have that information.

"Lee, I – "

Lee held his hand out to her. Jacey raced down the stairs, threw herself into Lee's arms and wept with all her heart. When he finally lifted her chin to face him, Lee kissed her tenderly, lingering for effect. Then, drawing apart, Lee said, "I'll talk to you tomorrow, Katie. Goodnight, love." Affectionately, he placed a hand against her cheek and stared into her eyes. She alone knew what he was saying. *You can do this, Jacey. Just turn around and go upstairs. Nothing more needs to be said.*

Jacey turned and dashed back upstairs, closing the door quietly behind her. She did not return to the main floor the rest of the night.

* * * * *

Lee and Jacey's demonstration of affection worked its magic. Although Rob visited Katie Chester and the Forbes several times, he never came when Lee was around. On his visits, Rob was cordial, but there was a coldness to him that had not been there previously.

Jacey's face had nearly healed and only a little tenderness remained. However, she had not been able to leave Scotland yet, as Lee had suggested. Court trials take weeks, sometimes months, and the case against Myles Chester did not seem to be hurrying along as Jacey anticipated. She knew the FBI was waiting until the last legal moment to spring Katie's testimony upon the court, and that could take time. Meanwhile, Jacey continued her undercover role as Katie Chester, even though she was prepared to leave the moment it was revealed to the court that Katie would appear as a witness for the prosecution.

If anyone at Forbes Manor thought it odd that Katie had not telephoned her father from a landline once since her arrival, Jacey did not worry about it. The FBI had an untraceable cell phone link from Forbes Manor to Katie, and the real Katie made regular calls to her father, further proving her loyalty to the Chester fortunes. After each call, Jacey was notified of the conversation, and she would try to mention the telephone visit next day to at least one of the Forbes family members. She could only hope they assumed she had called Myles Chester from her cellular phone.

In a few more weeks, *or months*, Jacey could return to San Francisco, where her father was still a patient in a rehabilitation program. He'd been sober for six weeks, and the worst hurdle – sobering up– lay behind him. Perhaps this time he would finally choose to be himself, the man she grew up admiring before her mother passed away. Reports on her father's progress arrived at Galashiels operations headquarters every week, and Jacey welcomed these reports with enthusiasm and hope.

Still, her heart ached for Rob. What had blossomed between them could not be denied, but it had to be quashed while Jacey remained undercover. Jacey forced herself to laugh brightly at Rob's jokes, listen to his tales, always with Rachel sitting between them. If Jacey seemed pale or withdrawn, and it was brought to her attention, she simply mentioned her concern over her father's trial, and nothing more would be said. But, in her heart, she knew the real problem was her continuing affection for Rob. How long she could go on pretending like this, Jacey had no idea. She only knew that she must not fail the undercover assignment she'd been given.

July passed quickly and Jacey found August upon them. During a casual breakfast, Jacey and Rachel lounged around the table in their housecoats, whispering and giggling. Rachel's exuberance was contagious, and Jacey suspected that Rachel was falling as hard for Lee as Jacey had for Rob. Miriam attempted to shoo them off to get dressed for the day, but they were both in a mood of lazy chatter and wouldn't budge. It was so out of character for Jacey, who really needed a good run each morning. But, Katie would probably be more flexible, and that was the only glue keeping Jacey in the kitchen chair.

While Miriam went upstairs to oversee the maids who were making the beds, the telephone rang and Rachel hurried off to answer it.

The sun shining through the bright kitchen curtains was warm against Jacey's back. The heat felt good and relaxed her tense muscles.

"That was the strangest call," Rachel said as she walked back into the breakfast room a moment later, shaking her fawn-brown hair off her shoulders.

"Oh?" Jacey responded, feeling drowsy in the warm morning sun.

"Some man wanted to know if this was where Katherine Chester lived. I answered that you were here on holiday and asked if he would like to speak with you. He said, 'No, thank you,' and hung up."

A sickening fear crept into Jacey's stomach. Had Myles Chester sent private detectives to check up on his daughter? Was it time to clear out? Would Chester stop at nothing to find Katie and silence her?

"I said, does anyone else know you're here?" Rachel asked, apparently for the second time, breaking into Jacey's thoughts.

"No. My father asked me specifically not to tell anyone my whereabouts." Jacey's mind raced overtime. Surely Lee and the other agents knew about the telephone call. They had, no doubt, already put a trace on it.

"I wonder who it could have been," Rachel said, sitting in the wicker chair opposite Jacey.

"Probably another suitor," Jacey quipped. *Sure, like I'm buried in them.* "You know, Rachel, I really need a good run. Do you want to join me today?"

"Oh, I suppose I must," she agreed. "But, I'm surprised Lee isn't here yet. He said he'd join us."

"Knowing Lee, he's probably off on some business deal or another." Jacey stretched, hoping she looked unrushed. "You know, you could wait for him. I don't mind running on my own. I do it in New York all the time."

"Would you mind terribly?" Rachel asked.

"Rachel, you don't need to run every morning just because I do."

"Thanks," Rachel grinned. "I think I'll go get dressed up for Lee. Do you think he'll notice?"

"If he doesn't, I'll be surprised," Jacey said, walking down the hall. When she thought it reasonably prudent, she dashed upstairs and pulled on the charcoal gray sweats she had stuffed into a drawer in the night stand in her bedroom. Then, she strapped a belt to her waist that not only hid some cash, her passport and her satellite phone, it holstered her Glock 24 handgun and an extra seventeen-round clip. It also left a little bulge, which worried Jacey.

Rachel was running a bath, Miriam and the maid were in Master Forbes' room, and the unknown caller was probably right outside, watching the house with binoculars. Silently, Jacey slipped downstairs and out through the front door, hoping whoever was looking for her would spot her and follow, which would draw them away from Rachel and the rest of the Forbes' household. She trudged bravely around the house, praying she had been spotted, hoping the unknown caller had her within his sight. Considering her obvious belabored trek from the front of the house to the rear, she decided whoever was after her could not have failed to see her. Convinced her pursuer would have to be blind not to have seen her yet, Jacey started running at her fastest pace, past the stables and toward Lake Thistle.

When she thought she was out of earshot, she started talking aloud, "Code 7! Code 7! This is KC2 to base. Someone called the house. Repeat, an outsider called the house."

Along the route, she opened her cell phone, pressed an automatic dial button, then attached the phone to her waistband, and pushed a hearing device into her ear. The moment she heard someone answer, she said, "This is KC2 to base."

"Copy that, KC2. KC3 is looking into it right now. Stand by for a possible pick up."

"I am southbound, repeat, southbound. Will continue course until you advise."

"Copy that, KC2. We are standing by."

Jacey continued running, unwilling to slow down for a moment. Adrenalin surged through her. A moving target is more difficult to hit, and she knew it only too well. As she ran, she zigged and zagged, first left, then right, repeatedly. By the time she reached the path that turned off to the dock, she heard a voice through her ear microphone. "KC2, the bird is in the air. I repeat. The bird is in the air."

"Copy that. KC2 is ready to rendezvous." Jacey continued running. Something was seriously wrong, otherwise, Lee would not have sent the helicopter after her.

Three minutes later, she sensed more than heard the powerful blades of the chopper and she ran off the trail toward the lake. At the water's edge, she saw the helicopter whirl up over the dale, and she continued running south until the helicopter had circled around and headed back toward her. She had only practiced this maneuver twice, but she had passed both times.

As the helicopter dropped down next to her, it continued its forward movement, slowing only slightly. Jacey saw her opening and jumped into the welcome arms of an agent at the brief second when her window of opportunity seemed secure. On entering, she banged her knee on the doorframe.

"Welcome aboard, Agent Munroe," yelled the burliest helicopter crewman she had ever seen.

"Glad to be here," she burst out. Just hearing her own name was a welcome relief.

The helicopter whisked its way over a southern hill and took her around several knolls, using evasive strategy, until the pilot received clearance to put Jacey down. Finally, they went straight to the airport, slowed long enough for her to disembark and dash into a small warehouse where she was to wait for further instructions, then the helicopter swept away into the late morning sky.

Chapter Eight

Several minutes later, Lee showed up carrying a shoulder bag. He was accompanied by two agents in finely tailored suits whom she had never met before, and two other men in bullet-proof vests, who were carrying weapons. With no introductions, Lee said, "Flowers arrived at the house about fifteen minutes after you were picked up. The deliveryman is being interrogated as we speak."

"How did Lord Chester find out?" Jacey asked.

"We don't know that, yet," Lee qualified. "But, you're out of here on the next jet. We have one fueling for you right now. Single pilot, six passenger seats, but only one of them besides yours will be occupied," he said, giving her a wink. "Remove your contact lenses and put these clothes on." Lee handed her the bag.

Jacey went behind a chalkboard to gladly remove her contact lenses and change her clothes. Apparently, the warehouse was used as a classroom for training pilots. Within a few seconds, she was back by Lee's side, dressed in a pair of black slacks and a black silk shirt. She felt like her stomach was twisted into a dozen knots, but the adrenalin rush kept her fully alert.

"I brought some black hair color," Lee said, giving her a paper bag. "Can you do it yourself after we get you aboard?"

"I'll do my best." Jacey took the small bag from him.

"Agent Munroe," said the younger of the agents. She couldn't quite read his name badge, as his lapel covered part of it. "Here's your new passport. You are no longer Katie Chester."

Jacey smiled, but her happiness was short-lived.

"You're still not Agent Munroe, either," said the older of the two. His name badge clearly identified him as Special Agent DuWayne Connelly. "You're now Natalie Parkinson. We're going to sneak you on the plane through the luggage compartment. Once you're aboard, work your way into the lavatory and lock yourself in, even for take-off. Until that plane's in the air, we won't breathe easy down here. We've got one of the Bureau's pilots flying you to Edinburgh. Once there, you'll find more documents and clothing in this locker." He handed her a key.

Jacey took it and nodded. She knew the procedure from the pilot's point of view, and hopefully that would be enough. The other agent apparently misunderstood her slight hesitation.

"Does he need to draw you a map of the airplane, Ma'am?" asked the younger man.

Lee burst out laughing. "She's a pilot for the Bureau, Agent Hill."

"My apologies, Captain Munroe," said Agent Hill, but Jacey noticed a crinkled frown cross briefly over his face.

"Apology accepted, Agent . . . Hill, is it? " Jacey smiled as he uncovered his name badge. "But, I haven't made captain status yet. I had planned on pursuing that goal when this assignment ends."

"I'm sure you'll do well," Special Agent Connelly encouraged, dismissing Agent Hill's comments entirely.

Jacey nodded. "Thank you, sir. Permission to sit in the cockpit once we're airborne?"

"I believe the pilot will be expecting you," said Special Agent Connelly.

"I'll notify the pilot personally," volunteered Agent Hill, and he slipped away from them, evidently to carry out this self-assigned duty.

A side door opened and a man in Scottish military uniform said, "Your transport is coming."

"Quickly, Jacey," said Lee. "I'll see you in the States." He shook her hand formally, as did Special Agent Connelly.

Jacey didn't have time to say goodbye. She raced to the door, saw a luggage carrier being driven right by the warehouse, noticed an opening on one of the carts and dived between three suitcases, pulling a loose tarp over her in one swift motion, leaving a small space from which to watch where the luggage carrier was going. In the farthest space on the tarmac, a Learjet 60 was disconnecting from a fuel umbilical. The carrier neared the plane, shielding anything between itself and the airplane. Since the plane's lower hatch was open, the moment the carrier was close enough, Jacey slipped from her position and jumped up into the plane's cargo hold, pulling the door shut and latching it securely from the inside. Then, she worked her way forward around several boxes until she reached the wall that separated the cabin from the luggage compartment. Cracking the door panel slightly, she noticed no one aboard yet, so she waited until she saw the Captain make his way up the exterior stairs. When he boarded, he looked back in her direction, nodded toward her even though he could not have seen her, then he turned and went forward, closing the cockpit door behind him. Apparently, she was assigned as the secondary pilot, because no other pilot entered.

Jacey took the primary pilot's nod as her signal to proceed to the lavatory. When she had reached and entered it, she closed the door and locked it. Immediately, Jacey mixed the hair color and applied it to her dry hair. She waited the customary time, then rinsed her hair in the sink, and dried it as much as she could with paper towels, then finger-combed her curls into a haphazard array. Still, the plane had not taxied to the runway, and she began to worry.

Finally, Jacey heard someone board the plane and take a seat in the cabin. While she waited, she stared at the woman in the lavatory mirror, a woman she almost recognized. Her golden-brown eyes were such a welcome relief from the green of Katie Chester. But, those awful curls! Black was no better than red, she decided. And, posing as Natalie Parkinson was still an undercover assignment. She had no idea when she would become Jacey Munroe again.

Within another five minutes, the plane was taxiing to the runway, and Jacey sank onto the commode lid and waited for takeoff. Soon, the plane was lifting safely into the air.

When Jacey felt the plane settle into its assigned airspace, she opened the lavatory door and received the shock of her life. Rob McLennan was the passenger who had boarded after the pilot!

Rob turned when she unlatched the lavatory door. His eyes widened in surprise, apparently at Jacey's change in appearance. Black slacks and silk shirt, indigo hair wet as rain, and her own brown eyes for once. Rob stood and took Jacey by the hand, leading her to the seat upon which he had been sitting. Wearily, she sank upon it, speechless.

"Katie," he said, filling the silence between them. "What is it?"

Jacey could not find her voice.

"Say something," Rob insisted, sitting across the aisle from her, facing her. When she didn't, he explained, "Lee gave me permission to come with ye."

Why? she wondered. Apparently, her eyes asked the question for her.

"Because I saw the helicopter rescue ye. I called Lee to find out what was happening, and he said –"

Jacey shook her head. Lee would not betray her like this. How could he? She had trusted him.

"What is it?" Rob asked. "Why are ye frightened?" Apparently, her face gave him a clue.

"Ye are afraid of me?" he whispered. "But, why?"

Tears slipped from her eyes, but she did not stop them. Rob had deceived Lee somehow. It could not be the reverse. She had trusted Lee with her life.

Suddenly, the tumblers fell into place in her mind. Finally, Jacey understood. *Rob sent the flowers!* He put her rescue into play to get her back to the States where Katie's father awaited her. Anger at Rob's keen betrayal scorched her mind and chilled her trembling heart. It was Rob all along.

Well, his plan wouldn't work. Rob had no idea who Jacey was, nor where she lived.

"Tell me what's wrong?" Rob pleaded.

Finally, she found her voice. "When did you speak to my father?" she asked, pleased that she sounded as cold as the ice in her heart.

"A few days ago. I was very discreet," he insisted.

Jacey stood up, drew her passport from her pocket and threw it in his face. "Well, it won't work!" she yelled, watching the horror in his eyes as he looked at the passport. "I'm not Katie Chester. I'm Natalie Parkinson. I was working undercover as Katie, helping her escape the one man who's been trying to bury her. You won't be bringing Katie Chester back to her father, as you and he planned. She's unavailable at the moment."

Rob stood so that she had to look up at him to read his expression. For a moment, she saw tenderness in his blue eyes, and confusion that was quickly replaced by anger.

Turning away, as though she wanted nothing more to do with him, she waited until she heard him sigh and whisper, "Katie, I– "

Thud! Instantly, Jacey had swung around and, using all her body weight, smashed the palm of her hand into his eye with a loud smacking noise.

Although dazed, Rob's reflexes were excellent, he grabbed both her wrists to stop her from hitting him a second time. Using the force of his pull against her, she lifted herself up and slammed her shoe against his groin with her full weight.

Rob released her, yelled in agony and fell forward onto the cabin sole. Jacey adapted another strike mode and waited for his reaction.

He pulled himself up onto a seat and held out his hand in protest. "Enough," he gasped. "I won't fight ye, Kat –"

"It's Natalie!" she challenged. "Try to get it right next time." Jacey grabbed her passport from the floor where it had fallen in their scuffle, and stuffed it into her back pocket. Rob reached for her, but she swiftly pulled out her handgun and pointed it at him. "Stay where you are!" she commanded.

Suddenly, the plane lurched and veered recklessly to starboard. Jacey was caught off balance. Rob wrestled the gun from her hand, but she kicked it out of his own and it went flying backward and landed by the lavatory door. While Rob went for the gun, Jacey instinctively lunged for the cockpit door. Tugging on the door with a firm jerk, she was disconcerted to learn the pilot had locked it from the inside. The plane continued to tilt to the right, and Jacey knew they were in desperate trouble if she couldn't get inside the cockpit.

"Shoot me and we both die," she said to Rob as he came toward her with the gun. "The plane's going to crash if you don't put my weapon down and help me get this door open."

Rob removed the bullet clip and tossed it behind him, then placed the gun, handle first, in her hand. "I have no intention of shooting ye," he moaned, "and no intention of ye shooting me, either. Step aside."

For once, Jacey did as she was told. Rob kicked on the cockpit door three times until the latch broke. Jerking the door open, she saw the pilot slumped over in his seat.

"What's wrong with him?" Rob asked.

"He's unconscious," she cried, stuffing the gun back in its holster behind her, exposing the other clip she could use if the need arose. She watched Rob gulp, but he did nothing further to antagonize her.

Jacey grabbed the pilot's shoulders and tilted him backward. Reaching over him, she took hold of the controls and steadied the plane, then switched on the autopilot. "Help me move him," she demanded, "or we all die!"

Rob reached into the cockpit and dragged the pilot out into the cabin aisle. As he did so, Jacey sank into the pilot's seat, kicked a half-empty bottle of spring water out of her way, buckled herself in and yelled back to Rob. "Keep him alive until I get this plane on the ground!"

"You're going to fly this plane?" Rob asked incredulously. "Ka– Natalie, do you know how to fly this airplane?"

She heard the concern in his voice and called back to him, "Yes, I do." Then, to get his mind off her flying, she yelled, "Check his pulse, make sure his airway is open."

Unable to assist Rob any further, she flipped on the transmitter and said, "Mayday! Mayday! Mayday! This is a Learjet 60, requesting emergency landing at Galashiels Airport."

Instantly, she received a response, "Learjet 60, this is Galashiels Control. State your emergency."

"My pilot has collapsed. He's unconscious." She paused in her report and glanced back at Rob.

"I can't get a pulse, his lips are blue," Rob said.

"Then start CPR, McLennan!" she demanded. "He's in your hands now." Relaying the message back to control, she said, "The pilot's cyanotic. CPR is being started now. "

"Who's flying the plane?" asked the control man. "Where is the secondary pilot?"

"My name is Natalie Parkinson. Please contact U.S. Special Agent Lee Carrington. I am sending his telecommunications data now." She tapped the number into the keyboard and pressed the send key.

"Ms. Parkinson, do you know how to land the plane?"

"Yes, sir. Just get me a clear runway and an ambulance. Now!" she barked, knowing Lee would clear her immediately, and be waiting the moment she touched down.

In the background, she could hear Rob performing CPR on the pilot.

The control tower personnel moved swiftly after that. She was soon directed to the correct altitude and given clearance to land. Jacey guided the plane to a safe touchdown, taxied onto the tarmac, came to a full stop and waited for the chocks to be set. Several ambulances and fire trucks met the plane, as did three black, unmarked sedans. The Scotland border patrol, in full military gear, escorted the emergency vehicles to the stairs, which were quickly put into place. Rob continued to work on the pilot while Jacey opened the side door and secured it.

Immediately, the patrol officers boarded the plane, weapons drawn. As soon as they saw it was clear, the paramedics were allowed up to continue the pilot's life support measures and rush him to the nearest hospital. When the pilot was in medical custody, Special Agent Connelly, Agent Hill and Lee Carrington boarded the plane.

Rob was sitting on a seat in the cabin, exhausted from his CPR duties. His left eye was swollen and bruised. He glanced up at Jacey, a question in his eyes. *What now?*

Jacey looked squarely at Lee and said, "Take this man into custody, Agent Carrington."

A puzzled frown crossed Lee's forehead. "Why? What's he done?"

"He admitted to me before the pilot collapsed that it was he who spoke to Myles Chester a few days ago." She glared at Rob, hating him for what he'd done.

Lee's mouth dropped open in surprise. Special Agent Connelly wasn't as slow on the uptake. "Take him to interrogation," he ordered two of the border patrolmen.

Agent Hill stepped backward, into the cockpit area, to get out of everyone's way. They swiftly placed Rob in handcuffs and took him away. Rob, apparently stunned by all that transpired, remained speechless.

"Nice landing, Agent," said Connelly. "But, you do present us with another dilemma. The whole of Scotland knows who and where you are."

"They know me as Natalie Parkinson," she debated. "For now, that's who I am."

"Does Mr. McLennan know who you really are?" Agent Hill asked, coming back into the cabin aisle, a bulge in his jacket pocket. He had apparently picked up the water bottle, and would take it to a lab to test it for poisons.

"You think I'd tell him my real name after what he's done?" she demanded.

Agent Hill raised his hands. "Don't bite me," he teased. "I didn't mean to offend you."

"I showed him my new passport to throw him off his game. He thought he was taking Katie Chester back to Daddy. I wasn't going to give him the satisfaction."

Shrugging, Agent Hill started to say, "Good–"

But, Connelly interrupted. "Good work," he said. "In the meantime–"

"Agent Munroe will stay with my team," said Lee. "I won't let her out of my sight."

"Chester's men will be looking for her. Take a full detail with you."

"We'll stay at the Crow's Nest," said Lee. "It's atop a knoll just outside Galashiels, surrounded by open fields and the view goes on forever. Agent Hill, take care of it. No one in, no one out."

"Yes, sir," said Agent Hill, stepping down the stairs ahead of them.

"We'll be sitting ducks," quipped Jacey.

"No," said Lee. "It's like a fortress. I've already assessed it as a possible safe-house. The owner is very discreet."

By the time Jacey was seated in one of the sedans headed out of town, it was early evening, her adrenalin rush had subsided and she felt wasted. Wearily, she rested her head on the back of her seat and fell asleep.

Several hours later, Jacey came screeching awake from a nightmare, jerking forward in her seat. The car was parked at the foot of a large hill graced with a Victorian manor atop it. The stately old manor was lit up with little white lights everywhere, like Christmas Eve.

"Where are we?" she asked.

"At the Crow's Nest entrance. I sent Agent Hill and the others up to scout the area and secure our position before I move you up there," Lee explained.

Jacey rubbed her eyes. "It's dark out. How long have I been asleep?"

"A few hours. We're still waiting. We want to move you in under cover of darkness."

"Thanks," she said, "for letting me sleep."

"You've had a busy day," whispered Lee.

As soon as she realized it was just the two of them in the car, and no one else was within earshot, she tried to focus on the man who had ripped her world apart. "What will happen to Rob?" she asked.

Lee shook his head. "I don't know. They'll let him sweat it out for about twenty-four hours before they start questioning him. But, I'll be honest with you, Jacey. I don't think he knew he was putting you in danger by talking to Chester. He was frantic when he saw you being rushed away today in the helicopter."

"That's another thing," she snapped. "If he saw me get into that helicopter, it had to be with binoculars. I was watching every angle, all the perimeter areas. I never saw him."

"He was in the stables when you ran past," explained Lee. "He called me from the stables."

"What was he doing there?" she asked. "Stalking me?"

"He's been helping the veterinarian with Storm. On the days I've been with you and Rachel, he's retreated to the stables. The guy's a wreck over what happened to the stallion . . . and if I'm not mistaken, over what we did to him."

"We did nothing to him," she insisted.

"We broke his heart when we kissed on the stairs that day," whispered Lee. "I should never have allowed it. You have no idea how miserable he's been."

"Miserable enough to call Myles Chester and put my and Katie's lives on the line," she said, unforgiving and unrepentant.

"All I'm saying is I don't think he knew it would come to this," Lee insisted. "He called from the stables, begged me to let him go with you on that plane. I knew he was hurting, I knew how you felt about him. I considered my gesture a going-away present."

"Some present," she hissed. "For a moment, I thought the betrayal came from you. Now, I see that you're just as gullible as I was when it comes to Robert Roy McLennan."

Chapter Nine

After Rob was taken into custody, Lee telephoned Rachel and asked her to pack a small bag and go immediately to stay with MayBelle McLennan, Rob's aunt. Jacey considered this a kind gesture on both their parts, and was grateful Lee had thought of it.

In the meantime, the safe-house was wired and every angle was covered by remote-fed cameras. For three days, Jacey was not allowed outside the Crow's Nest, and she was not made privy to telephone calls that Lee received, either. She was also informed that the pilot had been poisoned, but that he would survive.

Because she could not run outdoors, Jacey spent a lot of time running in place, and dashing up and down the stairs and hallways of the old mansion, which absolutely annoyed Agent Hill.

Occasionally, she looked out windows where the blinds allowed a small amount of light in, but this practice was strongly discouraged, especially by Agent Hill, who seemed to have developed a particular dislike for her. No one else looked out windows, either. They sat around a table loaded with small television monitors and watched silent displays.

The words to the song, *The End of the Road*, which Rob had taught her the day they rode horses together kept racing through her mind, and she ran to remove it, but inside the Crow's Nest, she couldn't make any headway.

Lee stayed nearby Jacey in sixteen-hour stretches. Only his most trusted agents were allowed to compensate for the brief times he could not guard her. Because of Agent Hill's growing animosity toward her – he seemed to blame Jacey for everything that had happened – he was not allowed to take Lee's place.

On the fourth day of confinement at the old mansion, Lee arbitrarily decided it would be safe enough to take Jacey with him on what he called a road trip, explaining he wanted to give her some space away from the other men. Relieved to be allowed outside, Jacey wondered why Lee did not say specifically where they were going.

However, when Lee drove the sedan toward the McLennan Estate, she rebelled. "Why are we going to Rob's?"

"I need to see Rachel, and you need to tell her your part in it."

"Why is Rachel still at Rob's?"

"It's safer at Rob's than at Forbes Manor."

"Why do I need to tell Rachel my part? Won't she believe you?" Jacey asked.

"She does believe me," Lee explained, "but she asked to see you. Don't you realize Rachel loves Katie Chester, like a dear friend?"

"She doesn't even know Katie Chester," Jacey responded. "She hardly remembers Katie from their one brief visit when Katie was seven."

"You have ears, but you do not listen," he mused aloud. "Rachel wants to say goodbye to the Katie Chester she does know."

Jacey sighed, admitting to herself that it must have worried Rachel when Jacey was whisked away from the Forbes Estate. Still, there was Rob to consider. "What about Rob? Won't he be there?"

"They had to release him, Jacey," Lee explained. "It wasn't Rob who hired the florist. They tracked that man down to a hotel in Melrose. He's a hit-man who slipped away before our people got there. We've found no trace of him."

Absorbing this much information, Jacey countered, "So, for all you know, he's still out there, looking for me."

"He could be," Lee admitted, "but we haven't seen any evidence of it."

"Then why take me from the safe-house?" she demanded, angry that he still hadn't considered Rob's role in the betrayal.

"Because I promised a friend," he confessed, looking away from her as he drove the sedan.

"You promised Rob you would bring me to see him?" she guessed.

Apparently, her summation was accurate because Lee nodded his head slightly, then gave her a brief grimace.

Trembling with rage, Jacey yelled. "How dare you! I will not speak to Rob McLennan again, if it's the last thing I do. He nearly got me killed."

"You can stay in the car, if you choose," said Lee, "but he'll only come out and join you. He's determined that you understand his side."

"His side," she moaned. "You're leaving my life in his hands, what a joke. He nearly got himself and the pilot killed. Even if his call to Myles Chester was innocent, which I doubt, he put my life at risk, and I want nothing more to do with him."

"Then, you should tell him that yourself."

"I thought I'd made that perfectly clear on the plane."

"You didn't talk to him, you attacked him. There is a difference, Jacey."

"You are a terrible matchmaker, Lee."

"I'm not trying to hook you two up, I'm trying to undo what I did to him, what we both did."

"You want me to share some blame in forcing Rob to face the fact that I won't be here for him to bully around any longer?" she asked.

"He had stopped bullying you long before we deceived him," Lee reminded. "You said you couldn't take any more temptation, so what you really wanted to do was to take away Rob's hope that he stood a chance with you. And, I agreed to go along with it."

"You're twisting the way it happened. I knew he was falling for me, but it wasn't really me, it was a woman he knew as Katie Chester. How could that ever work out if he loves Katie when I'm Jacey? And now, he knows me as Natalie Parkinson, so if he falls in love with her, it's still not me." She pouted and gave a weary sigh. "Besides, my feelings for Rob tarnished a few days ago." She pulled a lock of ebony curls away from her face.

"You're telling me you don't love him?" Lee asked. "Because, that would change everything I'm trying to do to help you two."

"Please stop playing Cupid, Lee," she pleaded. "You think I want a romance with someone who disregards my feelings and my safety, someone who can't come to me on his own steam, but needs to be led around by a matchmaker?"

"Tell me you don't love him and I'll back off completely," Lee promised.

Jacey frowned. The jury of her emotions was still out on her love for Rob. She had refused to let those feelings surface since she had placed herself in the Captain's seat aboard the Learjet 60, regardless of the song swirling around in her head. "Rob needs to realize I'm going back to America just as soon as it's safe to do so, no matter who I am. Nothing he says or does will prevent that."

"You failed to mention if you love him," Lee said, driving onto the circular, cobblestone drive-way in front of McLennan Hall, setting the brake and turning the engine off.

"You're forcing me to open old wounds to see if they still bleed," she complained. "They will. I don't have to open my heart up to know what's in it."

"So, you still have feelings for Rob?" he asked pointedly.

Jacey searched her heart and felt it fill up, all the way to her tear ducts, which flooded over until she could do nothing but weep softly. Lee pulled her into the circle of his arms and waited for her crying to subside.

After a while, Jacey dried her tears on Lee's offered tissue, and pulled down the visor to study her face in the mirror. Her eyes were red and puffy. Rob would know she'd been crying.

Lee reached out and turned her around to face him. "I'll send Rachel out to speak with you first. You can talk to Rob afterward. Perhaps, that will give your eyes a chance to clear." He reached into his pocket and pulled out a battered bottle of Clear Eyes. "Tilt your head back," he directed.

Jacey complied and he squirted a drop of the clear liquid into each of her eyes. It stung, but she knew it would help. "Thanks. I'll go wait in the rose court."

"Before you go, Jacey," said Lee, "you should know it was Master Forbes who telephoned Katie's father the night Storm broke his ankle. It was Forbes who told Chester his daughter, Katie, had been spending time with Rob McLennan, told him how she had set Rob's ankle and Storm's, how calm Katie had acted when faced with danger. He was worried Chester would see it on the news and worry needlessly. Chester knew Forbes wasn't describing his daughter, so he located Rob and called him to find out what he could about the woman posing as Katie Chester. Rob wouldn't give him the time of day."

While Lee went into McLennan Hall, Jacey walked down the cobblestone path to the rose garden, filled with sunshine, surrounded by sweeping lawns and lush, thick sycamore trees. Her thoughts focused only on Rob, and what he must think of her after she hit him, kicked him, and threatened him with a weapon. He must hate her by now.

Within moments, Rachel joined her, embracing Jacey wholeheartedly. "I'm so glad to see you again," she whispered. "You scared the life out of me, Katie. Oh, I mean, Natalie."

"I apologize," said Jacey. "I had no intention of frightening you." She pulled away and they walked around the courtyard of roses.

"I know," agreed Rachel. "It's just, Rob and I were so worried. He came running past the house that day, nearly bowled over the gardener, and when I called him on his cell phone as he hopped in his Landrover and sped out of the driveway, he said you'd been abducted by some men in a helicopter."

"I'm sorry I couldn't tell you the truth," Jacey said. "It was important to keep the illusion of Katie Chester going so her father wouldn't find out where she really is."

"Lee told me. He said it was the phone call from that unidentified man that started the whole thing. If you hadn't run out of there when you had, you may have been killed. We may all have been killed." Rachel shuddered.

"The plan was to let my presence be known, then distance myself from the house and the people in it with the utmost haste. We knew whoever was after Katie would leave you alone, once they'd seen me retreating away from the house. The helicopter picked me up en route, near the lake. I don't know when I've been so scared," Jacey confessed.

"Why did you have Rob arrested?" Rachel asked. "He would never hurt you."

"It was a misunderstanding," said Jacey. "A precaution. You understand."

Rachel shook her head. "He's hardly said a word to us, but he talked to Lee on the telephone a few times. When he arrived home after being interrogated, he looked terrible. They beat him up, Natalie."

Jacey smiled. "His left eye, right?"

Rachel nodded.

"I gave him that," admitted Jacey. "It's a long story, Rachel, and one I cannot tell you."

"Federal agents have too many secrets," she chided. "It's frustrating to the people with whom you get involved."

"It's part of the job, Rachel." Jacey responded. "We have no choice. Lives are lost when secrets are exposed."

They reached a bench and sat down upon it. As they did, Jacey noticed Rob and Lee walking toward them. She cringed, torn between not wanting to see Rob ever again, thinking he must wish he'd never met her by now, and praying he could forgive her, love her, and they would never be separated again.

"I'll go with Lee back to the house. You'll need some time alone with Rob." Rachel stood up, grabbed Lee by the arm and led him quickly toward the house, never looking back at Jacey or Rob.

As Rob approached her, Jacey remained seated, her eyes focused on the cobblestone patio at her feet. Her insides played ping pong and her heart pounded fiercely within her chest. Jacey clenched her fingers around the edge of the bench as she waited for Rob to arrive at the bench alone.

Sitting beside her, Rob held off speaking to her until Lee and Rachel were in the house. Then, he turned Jacey to face him, his hands gentle upon her shoulders. Tilting her chin up, Rob gave her no option but to look at him. Jacey studied his sky-blue eyes, while he looked deep into hers.

"Golden brown," he whispered. "I love the color of your eyes."

"I'm sorry," she muttered, tears slipping down her cheeks. "I–"

Rob placed a finger against her lips to shush her and shook his head, the expression on his face betraying his feelings for her.

Jacey stared, transfixed and captivated by Rob's nearness. A moment stretched infinitely long. All those weeks of keeping herself at arm's length, wanting but not having, overpowered her.

She loved this man in front of her. She knew it, and by his expression, he knew it as well. He had saved the life of a fellow pilot-agent, and had returned her handgun, refusing to fight with her, those actions were obvious clues. And had the plane crashed, he would have died beside her. Why hadn't she realized that before? What was wrong with her?

Jacey looked into Rob's eyes and saw raw emotional upheaval. The haggard look on his face told her far more than words ever could.

Without considering consequences, Jacey threw herself into his arms and kissed him passionately, over and over again. Rob responded with hot flames of love and desire, accepting and wanting her as much as she wanted him. But, when she felt his hands pressing against her back, bringing her closer than ever before, Jacey stiffened.

They had hardly said a word to each other, yet they were ready to make love to one another in the middle of a bright, clear day, out in the open, on a bench in his rose garden. No. She couldn't do it, not like this. As much as she wanted him, she did not want their first time together to happen in public, with no confession of love between them, no spoken vows of commitment.

Sensing her withdrawal, Rob released her and stood up. "I'm sorry, Natalie. I forgot we are being recorded, chapter and verse."

"Not today," she admitted standing up to face him. "I'm no longer Katie Chester."

Rob smiled and stepped closer to her. Out of the corner of her eye she saw the reflection of the sun off something shaped like the barrel of a rifle in one of the sycamore trees. Startled, she whispered, "I don't want you to get the wrong idea, Rob, but we are being watched."

"Just not listened to?" he asked with a smile. "Ye think I care if anyone sees me kissing ye, lass?"

"Hold that thought," she insisted. "And do kiss me, but when you kiss me, keep your eyes open and turn me around so we can both look into the branches of your trees. I think we are being watched, but not by the Bureau."

His eyes widened in alarm. Pulling her into the circle of his arms, as though he could protect her from any high-powered rifle by putting his body between hers and a bullet, Rob kissed her tenderly. However, his focus was on bending her back just enough that he could look past her at the tops of the sycamores. Withdrawing his mouth only a fraction from hers, he whispered, "Three of them with guns."

Jacey whispered, "I count four in my direction." She kissed him once again and withdrew just enough to whisper, "If they had intended to kill me, they would have by now. Keep me in the circle of your arms, as close as you can, and let's kiss our way back to the house. I doubt they'll shoot at us if they've been ordered to keep me alive."

Rob started moving toward the house. To Jacey's relief, Rob kept her so close there was no airspace between them. As his lips caressed hers, she realized these kisses were nothing like those kisses on the bench. Rob was cautious, his eyes searching, his body always coming between her and the riflemen's crosshairs as they moved their way slowly to the porch, through a French doorway, and into the sitting room.

Lee and Rachel were apparently somewhere else in the big, old-brick manor house. Rob grabbed Jacey's hand and raced with her down the hall to the kitchen, where they found Lee and Rachel slicing up sandwiches and stacking them on a plate.

"We're going to skip lunch," Rob said, his breathing heavy.

"Did you make up?" asked Lee.

"Yes," said Rob.

"No," said Jacey at the same moment, removing her handgun from the belt beneath her waistband.

"Yes, but– " Rob began again.

"Snipers!" Jacey gasped. "Seven of them outside."

"I counted nine," corrected Rob. "One's by the sedan, and I thought I saw another's shadow near the porch."

Chapter Ten

"Do you have weapons?" Lee asked Rob.

"Hunting rifles, three of them."

"It won't be enough," said Lee, opening his satellite phone. He pressed an automatic dialing button and waited a second or two before he said, "We're trapped at McLennan Hall, surrounded by nine snipers. Hurry."

"They'll never make it in time," said a voice from the kitchen entry. A man entered, dressed in what looked like military fatigues, wearing a bullet-proof vest and a ski mask over his head.

Jacey swung around, pointing her handgun at the intruder.

"You plan on shooting me with that?" He laughed. Then, he barked to no one in particular, "Squad leaders, move in."

Although Jacey had passed her weapons handling and firearms shooting drills, she had not fired her handgun in months. Would her aim still be any good? And, if she hit him, how long before the house would be swarming with other snipers?

Just as these thoughts formed in her mind, she heard the pounding of footsteps on the porch, in the parlor, down the hall. Four more heavily-armed men entered the kitchen. The first man nodded toward her, and she understood his unspoken command. Jacey cautiously placed her weapon on the table. The moment she did, one man secured her weapon while the first man grabbed her and pulled her backwards, out of the house.

Jacey refused to struggle. It was obvious that she was the intended target, and they wanted her alive. In order to keep the intruders from hurting Rob, Rachel and Lee, she offered no resistance.

The thug threw Jacey into the front seat of a BMW convertible parked down the lane leading to McLennan Hall. Nearby were two cargo vans. He turned a key in the ignition and the car roared to life. Squealing away from the curb, he yelled, "Don't move and you just might live."

"What about my friends?" she demanded. "I'm going to need reassurance they're all right, otherwise you'll have to fight me every step of the way."

The man nodded, pulled a VHF radio from his vest pocket and pressed a button. "The girl is secure. Give the agent the phone and retreat. Quickly, before company arrives."

After he placed the radio back in his pocket, he picked up a cell phone from the seat and handed it to her. "Press star-3," he told her.

Jacey did as instructed. One ring later, she heard Lee answer the phone. "Yes."

"Lee, is everyone all right?"

"Yes," he answered. "They pulled back and they're driving off in two vans. Where are you?"

"I'm– "

"You're headed back to Daddy, Princess!" the man yelled as he took the phone from her hands and tossed it out of the car as they sped along. Jacey's mouth dropped open as she realized he thought she was Katie Chester . . . in disguise. She looked back and watched in the distance as the two vans began to follow them. Her mind raced ahead to the road they were on, and what curves, turns and escape routes she might remember ahead of her.

The car slowed down long enough for one of the vans to pull around in front of them, then they drove at top speed towards the Galashiels airport.

Traffic was sparse, which gave Jacey less civilians to worry about should there be an accident.

Neither Jacey nor her captor had put on a seat belt. This could work for her, or against her. From her memory, Jacey extracted a recollection of a bend in the road right before a bridge over the River Tweed. A good swimmer, Jacey knew if she could get control of the car at just the right moment, she might be able to survive a crash off the bridge.

As they drew nearer the airport, she pictured the bridge again and again in her mind, praying she remembered it correctly. Suddenly, she heard gunfire behind her. Looking back, she could see Rob's Landrover and Lee's sedan speeding toward the van, which was following the BMW in which Jacey was a captive. A helicopter was also overhead, swooping down upon them. Jacey knew the FBI would not fire on the BMW with her inside, so stopping her captor was going to be her responsibility.

"Don't get any ideas, Princess," warned the kidnapper. "Daddy wouldn't want his precious cargo hurt."

Looking down at his hand, Jacey noticed for the first time that he was holding a handgun and the barrel was pointed directly at her. She gasped.

The color blanched from her face, but her mind continued to race ahead to the bridge.

Someone in the helicopter was shooting at the van behind them with high-powered artillery missiles. Suddenly, the rear van burst into flames and exploded. This caused her captor in the BMW to curse and drive even faster and more recklessly, weaving in and out of traffic as if playing a video game where consequences were not life-threatening. The van ahead of them slowed, allowing the BMW to pass it, which was a fatal mistake, for the second van soon burst into a tower of smoke and debris from a well-aimed missile from the helicopter.

Jacey looked ahead to the curve in the road and the bridge that followed. She would have perhaps three seconds to deploy her plan at this speed. With no other avenue to pursue, she prayed the element of surprise would be to her advantage.

The bridge loomed closer, faster, as they entered the curve. Jacey looked back to see Rob's Landrover almost upon them, followed by Lee in the sedan. The driver of the BMW aimed his weapon at the Landrover and started firing. Jacey would have to act quickly, if Rob was to be spared.

As they started to come out of the curve, Jacey steeled her nerves. *Not yet*, she told herself. *Not yet.*

Suddenly, they reached the point of no return. *NOW!* screamed her mind.

Instantaneously, Jacey grabbed the steering wheel and pulled it hard to the left. The gun exploded near her right thigh. Her abductor cursed. The BMW smashed into the guard rail on the left, spun around twice and bounced over the guard rail on the right. An explosion sounded in her head and Jacey felt something warm running down her leg. The fall from the bridge seemed to take forever, as though happening in slow motion. As the BMW penetrated the water's surface, Jacey tried to jump out of the car, far enough away so that she would not be sucked under by the force of the sinking vehicle. But, to no avail, she was too slow and too late. Instantly, she felt the cold splash of water against her, the sucking of the car as it tried to pull her under, the silence of the river underwater. Struggling to swim upward, she realized her shirt was caught on some metal object on the door. She couldn't pull herself free, so she slipped out of the shirt and stroked her way up to surface, where the current drifted her gently to the side. Jacey tried to pull herself up onto the bank, but she couldn't think. Pain like she'd never known before screeched through her head. Weak and confused, she passed out face down before she could get completely out of the water.

* * * * *

"Jacey, can you hear me?" whispered an anxious voice near her ear. "Jacey!"

"Yes," she mumbled, but her voice sounded far away.

"It's Lee. Do you know who Lee is?" came the voice again.

Sorting through the mists in her mind, Jacey put a face to the name. She tried to nod, but it was too painful to move her head.

"Do you remember where you are?" he asked.

"Hospital," she muttered. "I'm in a room with . . . someone named Natalie."

Jacey heard Lee curse, and she forced her eyes to open. It hurt her head to do so, but she had to see if the voice really came from the face she'd put to the name he'd given her.

A blurry-faced man swam before her several seconds before coming into focus. Sun streaked across the room through the slats in the Venetian blinds at the window. Lee Carrington was sitting in a chair by her bed, whispering to her. "Jacey, you've been working undercover for the FBI, under the name Natalie."

"Oh?" she blinked, trying to remember. "Okay."

"Do you remember anything about the accident?"

Jacey closed her eyes and tried to focus. After a while, she remembered a BMW, a man in a mask, and the River Tweed racing straight toward her. With a start, Jacey opened her eyes again. "Yes. Is he gone?"

"The man in the BMW?" Lee asked.

Nodding, Jacey said, "Did we get all the bad guys?"

"All of them," said Lee.

For the first time, Jacey smiled, and found that it hurt to do so. Another memory formed in her mind, the face of a man with auburn hair and clear blue eyes. "Rob," she whispered.

"He's just outside," said Lee.

"Does he want to see me?" Her heart quivered inside her chest as other memories flashed before her . . . love, passion, betrayal and fear.

"He's been waiting five days to see you. The doctors haven't let anyone in but me. You were hurt pretty bad, Jacey. We nearly lost you."

"Sorry," she said as Lee wove in and out of focus. Then, as she drifted off to sleep, she said,

"Tell Natalie to listen to the doctors. She won't do anything they say."

The next time Jacey opened her eyes, it was dark outside. Her head felt like it was exploding with pain, but at least she could think more clearly now. Lee was holding her hand, rubbing it back and forth. She didn't have to focus at all this time, his face appeared right next to hers "Jacey!" he exclaimed. "Jacey, you woke up."

Blinking, she said, "How long have I slept?"

"Ten days," Lee admitted. "Jacey, we need to get you out of here. Do you understand what I'm saying?"

"Without seeing Rob?" she asked.

"You must pretend you don't recognize Rob. Do you understand?"

"Why? What's wrong?"

"Jacey, Rob and I were the only ones who knew you would be at McLennan Hall that morning."

"But, Rob protected me. He got me to the house safely."

"He also left the parlor door open so your captor could enter the house undetected."

"A mistake," she insisted. "Rob would never hurt me. Maybe there was a wire tap, or a phone tap, or a bug somewhere," she insisted, trying to think, trying to force life back into herself.

"We swept everything. There were no listening devices anywhere."

"But Rob . . . he loves me . . . doesn't he?"

Lee shook his head. "He may, Jacey, but he's still working with Katie's father. You were right. I was wrong to bring you to McLennan Hall. The whole time, I was wrong." His voice cracked and she heard the anguish in it.

"No," she said, turning her head from side to side even though the pain was ferocious.

"Worse," said Lee. "More of Myles Chester's thugs were spotted in Edinburgh this evening. They've rented two cars and are headed this way. We've got to move you tonight."

"I have to see Rob," Jacey insisted. "I have to say goodbye to him."

"No," scolded Lee. "He thinks you have amnesia, as do the doctors. You don't respond to anyone calling you Natalie. In fact, you haven't responded to anyone so far, but me."

"Lee, please. I have to see Rob. I can pretend I have amnesia. I've been a good actress once, I can do it again. Please, Lee," Jacey begged.

Finally, Lee relented.

"Your transport will be here in five minutes. After that, we've got to move you," he warned.

"Has he seen me yet?" she asked.

"No. We gave the doctors strict orders. No one in here but me or Special Agent Connelly. We're trusting no one else with your safety." Lee squeezed her hand. "I'll be right back," he said, then he left the room.

The next moment, someone took her hand again. Jacey opened her eyes and looked up into the sky-blue eyes of the man she loved, Rob McLennan, the man whom Lee said had betrayed her once again. Special Agent Connelly stood beside Rob, his hand on his sidearm, apparently for her protection.

When Rob said, "Hi, Natalie," it wasn't difficult to wonder who he was talking to, for Jacey knew exactly who she was, even if Rob didn't.

She gave him a puzzled expression in response.

Rob sank into the chair beside her bed. "'Tis good to see ye, lass," he said, his cheeks dimpling as he smiled. "Are ye in much pain?"

Jacey nodded. "My head– " she stammered. "My head hurts."

Just then, another man entered the room. He came over and stood on the other side of her bed. "Well, Natalie, is it? I'm Dr. Fordsham. They tell me you don't know who you are."

"Someone said Natalie. Is that right?" she asked, looking at the doctor.

"Yes, that is correct. Can you move your feet, Natalie?" he asked, and he lifted the sheet up to expose her ankles. A smile crossed his face as she slowly bent her toes, then straightened them. "And your hands?" the doctor prompted.

Jacey was still holding Rob's hand, so she clenched her other into a fist, and squeezed Rob's hand at the same time.

"Good, good," he gave his approval.

"Will I be all right?" she asked.

The doctor gave a nod to Special Agent Connelly. "Yes," he said. "You have a long road ahead until you're fully recovered, but in six months, you probably won't have any residual problems except the scarring, where the bullet entered and exited your lower right thigh."

"I was shot?" she asked, trying to remember.

Rob squeezed her hand, drawing her attention to himself as the doctor left the room. "Yes, Natalie, ye were shot, wrecked in a car crash and nearly drowned, all within seconds of each other. Do ye remember nothing?"

"Are you another doctor?" she asked.

"Natalie, 'tis me, Rob. Do ye not recall the trembling of your heart when I kissed ye? Can ye not feel anything for the man who loves ye?" A tear ran down his cheek.

She lifted her hand and wiped the tear away. "Rob?" she asked, wonderingly. "Do you love me?"

"I do, Natalie. That I do," he said, smiling broadly.

But when he called her Natalie, she remembered what she must do. "Who's Natalie?" she asked, giving him the finest performance of her life.

"Ye are Natalie," he insisted. "Natalie Parkinson. That day in the rose garden, sweetheart, I hoped we could begin to build a life together."

Tears welled up in her own eyes, but she used them to her advantage. "Who am I?" she whispered, hoping her voice sounded frightened. "Are you sure I'll be all right, doctor?" This question was directed to Special Agent Connelly.

The Special Agent put a hand on Rob's shoulder. "I don't think it's wise to give her too many facts, Mr. McLennan. The doctor said we could overload her, and that would push her memory farther away than it is already. We cannot risk that."

Rob nodded. Special Agent Connelly led him toward the door. "Go home, Mr. McLennen. We have your number. If there's any change, I'll call you."

"Thank you for letting me see her," Rob said as he left. But, Jacey heard the cracking of his voice that betrayed the emotional anguish he was suffering.

After Rob left the hospital, everything happened so fast Jacey scarcely had time to catch her breath. Lee arrived with a gurney. Dr. Fordsham and Agent Connelly assisted him in lifting Jacey from the hospital bed. A latex form was placed over her, with barely space for a breathing hole at her mouth. The form resembled the front of an obese old man covered with a bed sheet. There was a space beneath the latex form for Jacey to lie quietly. To any observers who might see the gurney, they would believe a heavy-set man was being moved.

Jacey, along with several pieces of hospital equipment, was wheeled down the hall to a waiting elevator. After the elevator ride, she was taken down another hall, then out into an ambulance. It wasn't until the sirens were screaming that the latex form was removed and Jacey found Lee Carrington smiling down at her. Beside him sat Dr. Fordsham, who had briefly examined her earlier in the hospital, and had assisted in moving her to the ambulance.

Dr. Fordsham felt her pulse, counted her respirations, adjusted the monitors to which she was still attached, and said, "This will be a very rough ride for you, Natalie. I'm going to give you something to help you relax."

"That's good," she whispered, "because I'm a little – "

Jacey remembered nothing afterwards. When she awoke again, she found herself in a Navy hospital in Bethesda, Maryland, and everyone was calling her Agent Munroe.

Chapter Eleven

Waking up in a world without Rob was more difficult than Jacey had ever imagined. Knowing he would never know who she was, or where she lived haunted Jacey like the compelling song Rob had taught her, *The End of the Road*. She came back to it over and over, replaying the song in her mind while trying to sweep the memory from her heart. But, the recollection never left her, not for one second.

When Jacey was finally scheduled to be flown to a physical rehabilitation center in San Francisco, she was amazed to find her father, Jake Munroe, waiting for her on the tarmac. She turned her head slowly and looked up into her father's golden brown eyes, from whom she'd inherited hers. His wavy, silver hair was swept to the side, and dark circles beneath his eyes made him seem older and more weathered.

"Dad?" she cried happily, tears staining her cheeks. "Is it really you?"

"Jacey, baby!" he exclaimed, kneeling in front of her wheelchair. He placed his cheek next to hers and held her hand with paternal concern. "You don't know what I've been through, worrying about you. When Mr. Carrington called to say you'd been in an accident, my whole world fell apart."

Jacey felt his tears mingle with hers and she realized Jake Munroe was actually crying. She hadn't seen him cry since the day her mother died.

"Dad, I've missed you so much." Jacey didn't know whether to laugh or cry, so she did both.

Jake confessed, "The past two weeks have been the worst weeks of my life, not knowing how you were. Mr. Carrington called me every day with an update, but it wasn't enough." Jake wiped her tears away, then his own. "Every time I closed my eyes, I saw some of the worst accident cases I handled in my earlier career, the patients' bodies mangled and dying, but the face was always yours. I guess we never realize how much we care until it happens to someone we love."

Needing to hear just those words, Jacey cried even more. "I love you, too, Dad. You don't know how badly I've needed to hear you say that."

"I know I haven't been the best father, Jacey, but I've always loved you. It's just that, you're so much like your mother. You may have my eyes, but everything else about you is Lucy. Even when you were younger, you were your mom in miniature." He choked on a few tears, then finally held them back and continued, "When your mother died so unexpectedly, I was devastated. All the medical knowledge and skill I had as a doctor and I couldn't save my own wife!" His voice cracked and he rested his head on her shoulder, and wept like a child.

"We're both survivors, Dad," she said, stroking his head. "We'll be all right now."

Her father nodded firmly, and Jacey noticed his dedication and focus had changed. He seemed to want nothing more than to help her body heal. He assisted her up the ramp and onto the small plane that would take her back to San Francisco. When she was seated and comfortable, Jake said, "You'll never guess the job I've got now. I'm working in physical therapy. I'll be at the center where they're sending you. It shouldn't take more than a week or two until I can move you back to the condo. You're going to be okay."

Jacey didn't want to ask, but she had to know. "And you, Dad? How are you doing?"

"Best thing that ever happened to me, Jacey, going into rehab for my addictions," Jake confessed. "I've been clean ever since. I got out three weeks ago, and your director gave me a good referral over at the P.T. Center. I'm helping young people learn how to walk again, after they've had an accident. Some of them are pretty sad cases, too. But, we keep at it day after day."

"I can walk, Dad. But, I damaged my right thigh in the accident. It doesn't work quite like it should. They say I'll be good as new in six months, though."

"Then, we'll keep working your thigh until it starts doing what you tell it to do, and we won't give up, baby. You never gave up on me, and I'm never going to give up on you." Jake tousled her curly black hair. "What's up with this?" he asked with a quirky grin.

"Don't worry," she encouraged. "I'm going to a see a hair stylist as soon as they release me. A professional will be able to restore it to my natural color."

"And the kinky curls?" he teased.

"I hate them," she laughed. "But, you should have seen them when they were red."

"Red? You dyed your hair red?" The surprise on his face was laughable.

"Undercover work, Dad. You know, I'd tell you all about it, but I'd have to shoot you," Jacey bantered.

They talked and she giggled nearly all the way to San Francisco. When the plane finally touched down, she was thrilled to see one of the agency's cars waiting to whisk her and her dad over to the Physical Therapy Center.

Early the next morning, Jake came by her bedroom and woke her up. "Come on! I've got a full day planned for you. I need to see how much range of motion you've got, and decide on a program to get your leg working."

It wasn't as bad as Jacey expected. She pushed herself harder than her father did, but that was her way. Who else would get up at five every morning to run four or five miles every single day? Jake had started her running program when she was just a young girl, and she loved it. Running was the one constant in her life.

Within two weeks, Jacey was able to go home, as Jake had promised. It wasn't easy learning to run again. Neither was it easy healing her broken heart. Her stylist restored her hair to its former golden-brown, and tamed the curls completely. But, Jacey wished someone could restore her heart to the way it was before her trip to Scotland. Reluctantly, she admitted that would never happen.

By mid-September, Jacey felt a big breakthrough in the way her right thigh was working. She didn't understand what it was, but her father explained that she was finally able to retrain her nerve endings to respond to commands from her brain. After that, her physical therapy took giant leaps forward. Two weeks later, Jacey started running through the park, along the route she had taken hundreds of times before.

She had not gone back to piloting planes for the Bureau, not yet. The FBI was giving her plenty of time to recuperate. Medical leave wasn't too bad, she could do anything she pleased and still get paid for it.

Of course, she still had to use caution, but no one had shown any interest in harming her since she returned home, and Lee Carrington was given other priorities in San Francisco, in addition to remaining in contact with Jacey Munroe.

As soon as she was permitted back on desk duty, Jacey began preparing for re-certification to keep her pilot's license and weapons qualifications. Because the problem with her early memory stemmed from the bang on her head when the BMW went over the guard rail, the Bureau would not clear Jacey for active duty until she passed every test again. Once she had recovered her former status as pilot and field agent, she could also apply for her Captain's license.

In order to pass her Captain's exam, Jacey spent extra time in a simulation module, flying around in cyberspace. Since she left her Glock 24 handgun at McLennan Hall, and was forbidden by the FBI to contact Rob, she bought a new Glock 27, which she took to the firing range every day. As she retrained her hands and eyes to coordinate with one another, Jacey's shooting ability quickly improved. In addition to these two activities, Jacey began working out with a personal trainer, who taught her improved self-defense skills. It was better than being at Quantico, Virginia, because she had a physical fitness program her trainer designed specifically for Jacey, which targeted her weak areas, then strengthened them.

In early October, Jacey was given the dates for re-certification, and she hoped she would be ready for every one of them. This time around, she wanted to pass them more than ever before. Constantly driving herself to excel prevented her from dwelling on Rob and how much she missed him. Nights were the worst, when she tossed and turned, trying unsuccessfully to sleep without Rob entering her dreams. Consequently, she dropped ten pounds and considered herself a nervous wreck.

A week before the exams began, Jake came home from work in a high-pitched frenzy of excitement. "I've got plane tickets to San Diego! A condo on the beach where you can run every morning. A barbecue grill right outside the back door, where we can listen to the ocean surf as we dine in the sunset. What do you say?"

At first, Jacey didn't know how to respond. She was so busy with exam preparations she couldn't spare the time, and she thought her father should have realized that by now.

Her father evidently understood her hesitation, but he was relentless, "You need to get away from all the pressure for a few days. We've hardly talked since you came home from the Center. Doctor's orders. Is that a yes I hear?"

Jacey could not say no. Besides, he was right. They hardly communicated at all now that she was working so hard to return to her life as a normal pilot and field agent while, at the same time, Jake remained busy at the P.T. Center. Life had drawn them apart this time, it had nothing to do with his drinking because he had remained sober since he left rehab.

"All right. When do we leave?" she asked, giving him a quick hug.

"Tomorrow afternoon," he said. "Get your clothes packed, Princess. This will be one trip you're never going to forget." He swung her around as they danced a little jig. Then, he twirled her away from him and laughed. "If your mother could see us now, I think she'd be proud, don't you?"

A smiled cracked Jacey's face. It was the first time her father had mentioned her mother with such a happy tone. "She can see us, Dad. I've always thought she watches over us."

"Then, she didn't do so good with me the last few years, but I forgive her. She was probably too busy looking after you." He nodded and went into his bedroom, whistling as he pulled a suitcase out of the closet.

Jacey felt her dad's exuberance wash over her in a rippling effect. His happiness was contagious, and she began to hope she could feel joyful once again. She also planned to talk with her father about Robert Roy McLennan. Jake's heart had apparently healed since her mother's death, and he might be able to help her learn how to heal her own heart.

Ever since she left Galashiels, Jacey had driven herself hard with every waking moment, and it wasn't just about re-qualifying for flying with the FBI. It was about leaving Rob without being able to tell him who she was, or where she lived. Leaving love behind her, choosing liberty instead of betrayal, logic instead of passion, these factors entered into her mental and physical well-being. Until she could reconcile herself to a future without Rob McLennan, she would never regain her reason for being.

* * * * *

The rented condo on the beach south of San Diego was exquisite, the sunsets magnificent. Wild ocean surf pounded and pulverized most problems into nothingness. Or, so it seemed until their final evening together.

On the horizon, the sun danced placidly above the water's edge, providing the last few rays of golden warmth for the day. They watched the sun kiss the ocean, sending ripples of light dancing toward them. It was the perfect sunset to a vacation she had only dreamed about in her youth.

Jacey had managed to start eating again, and had done very little but play card games with her father, build sand castles, and collect sand dollars that washed up on the beaches by the thousands in the fall. They took a day-trip to Sea World, but mostly, they surfed small waves right outside their own condo door.

Several days in the sunshine restored Jacey's tan to a golden sheen, and her heart began to mend a little. The last evening together, Jacey finally felt like sharing her feelings with the one man whom she knew really loved her. Granted, it wasn't the way a woman wanted a man to love her, but paternal love was as good as she was going to get at the moment.

"Dad, what was it like to be in love?" she asked.

It seemed her father had been waiting for her question, planning for it, because he had his poignant answer all ready. Jake rubbed her shoulders and began, "Your mother and I refused to let love get in the way of our careers, and it has only been in her absence that I've learned what love is all about.

"Love is more than just kissing, holding, fondling and embracing. Passion and fire, they enter in, but they are not all there is to love. There is also listening to the sound of someone's laughter, and knowing it is one of the most beautiful melodies you will ever hear. Love grows stronger with each passing moment, whether you're together or apart. Nothing can break real love when that is what you feel.

"Love is finding out your sweetheart left his house key at work and waking up for him when he rings the doorbell at one in the morning, after a full day of surgery ran into overtime, then rubbing his feet and laughing at the same jokes he's told you for fifteen years.

"Love is walking the floor with a colicky baby while your wife sleeps because she was up with her the night before. Love is carrying that child on your shoulders as you introduce her to an ice cream cone, knowing you'll have to wash your hair when you get home, but you make that sacrifice for your child so she can experience and enjoy life.

"Love is knowing your world can only be right when the person you love is with you. Love is forgiving someone when they've made a terrible mistake. But, you can't hate them because you love them, and you know it, so you keep on loving them regardless of their shortcomings."

Jacey smiled and turned to face her father. "I've known some of those feelings, Dad. I met a man while I was undercover in Scotland, and I had to leave him behind before I could tell him anything true about myself."

"Your assignment is over, Jacey. If you love him, perhaps you should go back to Scotland

and tell him how you feel." He arched an eyebrow knowingly.

"I can't. The reason why I went undercover . . . that situation is not resolved yet. It's still tied up in federal court. Until the trial is over, there's nothing I can do."

"You're certain that you love this young man?" Jake asked.

Jacey nodded. "My heart aches every second without him. I can't bring myself to focus on anyone but him, so I force myself into strenuous activity in order to forget him. But, his face never leaves my mind. I worry what he's doing, and I wonder if he misses me as much as I miss him. I have no right to love him, in fact, I know I shouldn't. I've tried not to," she admitted as tears formed in her eyes and dripped down her face. "I was advised by the agents still working on the case that I should never contact him, even when the trial is over."

Concern weathered her father's eyes when he asked, "Does he love you?"

"He said he did," she confessed. "But, it was when I was still coming out of the coma from the accident, and he may have said it just to encourage me to get better. If he really loved me, as he said, wouldn't he look for me? Wouldn't he find me somehow?"

"Did he ever know your name?"

"Not my real name, no."

"How is he supposed to find you when he does not know who you are?"

"I don't know. Besides, the other agents think he was the one who betrayed me."

"He betrayed you?" Grave concern peppered Jake's tone.

"But, I don't believe he did, Dad," Jacey insisted. "There has to be another explanation. They didn't see him when he was protecting me from snipers, putting his body between me and the gunmen. They didn't see the look in his eyes when he said he loved me, and hoped we could build a future together. I saw it in his eyes. I felt it in my heart."

"My advice," Jake said, stroking his chin thoughtfully, "is this: If you still feel certain about your love for this man when the case is officially closed, you should follow your heart, and forget what anyone else has told you."

"Thanks, Dad. I was hoping you'd say that."

"In the meantime," Jake interjected, "let me suggest something therapeutic for your soul. Write a letter to this man . . . you don't need to mail it, Jacey. Just write it. Expressing your feelings on paper can be very therapeutic."

Jacey leaned against her father's shoulder as he wrapped a strong arm around her. "Thanks, Dad," she whispered. "For everything." In her heart, Jacey knew her father understood she was saying thank you for more than his advice. She was thanking him for finally coming home.

Chapter Twelve

Later that night, after Jake went to bed, Jacey sat at the patio table, forming in her mind the things she wanted to tell Rob . . . to help him understand. After more than an hour of deliberation, she opened a box of stationery, slid several pieces of embossed paper onto the table and picked up her pen.

Dear Rob,

My name is Jacey Munroe, but you know me as Natalie Parkinson. Although I am an agent with the FBI, pretending to be Katie Chester was my first undercover assignment. Usually, I fly the Bureau's jets and other aircraft, taking agents all over the world.

I live with my father, Jake, a recovering alcoholic, so you can probably understand why I was upset to learn you had been arrested once for being drunk and disorderly.

My body has healed, yet I fear my heart will never mend. There were things I should have said to you at the hospital in Galashiels, Scotland. However, I was under a direct order to maintain my cover as an amnesiac. I'm sorry I had to deceive you.

After I left Galashiels, I woke up in a Navy hospital in Maryland. I spent three weeks there, then two more weeks in a physical therapy center in San Francisco where my dad works.

If Myles Chester's attorneys secure an innocent verdict at his trial, Katie Chester will probably fall victim to his hired gunmen regardless of the FBI's vast resources and protection capabilities, and my life will still be in danger, as Chester is consumed with vengeance, especially now that he knows his daughter plans to testify at his trial.

If Chester is convicted, his assets will be seized and he will be incarcerated for life, or perhaps given the death penalty. Hopefully, his conviction will give Katie an opportunity to live relatively safe, under the witness protection program. And, my life would return to normal, too.

I don't believe you deliberately betrayed me a second time, as Agent Carrington and Special Agent Connelly seem to think. I trust you, Bob. Your hope, as expressed in my hospital room, is my hope as well.

All information regarding me has been classified top secret by the FBI, so it will be almost impossible for you to locate me through normal channels. But, if you love me as you said, I pray you will find me.

Until that day, I shall never forget you. I can still hear the sound of your voice and the bagpipes you played for me last summer atop a Galashiels hill.

All my love,
Jacey Munroe

After reading the letter over a dozen times, Jacey realized she could not bring herself to send Rob the letter. It seemed too impersonal. No, the only way she could ever tell Rob how much she loved him would be face to face.

However, Jake Munroe was right. Just putting the words down on paper, pretending she had sent it to Robert Roy McLennan, did help her put some of the past behind her. As a final cathartic, Jacey went over to the gas grill and turned on the flames. One by one, she burned all three pages of her letter to Rob until there was nothing left of it but ashes, which were swept from the grill by a unexpected northwesterly breeze and taken out to sea. Sadly, the memory of what she had written Rob in the letter was burned into her heart forever.

* * * * *

The following week, Jacey passed all her exams with higher marks than she had three years previously. At the awards ceremony, where her father stood in applause with the audience while her stomach fluttered inside her, Jacey was presented her Captain's License and a gold badge with the seal of the FBI, including a handshake from Director Stevens, who had flown in especially to see her progress and to personally honor her. The thrill she received was unequaled by any experience, other than the memories of Rob's kisses the last time she went to McLennan Hall.

Two weeks later, glad to be back at work as a pilot and field agent for the Bureau, with a healthy increase in her income, she arrived home from a flight and heard her father, Jake, in the shower. Jacey pulled one of her mother's cookbooks out and dusted it off. Perhaps she would try something domestic tonight.

Thumbing down the cookie index she noticed her mother had circled a recipe called "Coconut Oatmeal Macaroons." Jacey opened to the page and studied the ingredients. She had everything in the kitchen except the coconut.

"Dad," she said, tapping on the bathroom door. "I'm going to run to the market for some coconut."

"Would you get some floss while you're there? We're out," came his request from behind the door.

"Okay, I'll be right back." She slipped into a pale, peach-colored jogging suit, put on her sneakers, pocketed her I.D. and some cash, then headed out the door. Thinking her father may call her with other items to put on the list, Jacey returned and grabbed her cell phone. The nearest grocer was only five blocks away, so Jacey started running up Moraga Avenue and turned right on Mesa Street. As she did, she noticed a black Ford Explorer with dark tinted windows slowly pull away from the curb and begin to follow her. She kept on running as it passed her and turned left on Keyes Avenue. By the time she reached Keyes, the Explorer was nowhere to be seen. Jacey sighed in relief, chastised herself silently for even suspecting she was being followed, and continued her trek toward the neighborhood market.

Once inside, Jacey picked up a bag of coconut flakes and a package of dental floss and went to the checkout counter. Outside, she saw the same black Ford sitting in a parking space across the street. *I'm not imagining it at all!* she thought wildly, wishing she had brought her Glock 27. She paid cash for her groceries, then stretched the handles on the plastic bag over her arm and up onto her shoulder. Taking her cell phone from her pocket, she turned it on vibrate and headed out the automatic doors.

Once she left the store, she had no protection, but Jacey wasn't about to endanger the lives of any other civilians. She stayed close to the buildings, and when she saw the opportunity to duck into an alley, she took it, ran partway down, and slipped inside a doorframe on the far side of a Dumpster.

Within three seconds, the Ford followed. Jacey hunched down behind the trash receptacle and waited, but the Explorer didn't come any farther than a few feet into the alley. The driver waited about three minutes without progressing any deeper. During that time, Jacey memorized the license plate number, and managed to get a photo of the Explorer with the camera in her cell phone, while stretched out on her stomach on the ground behind the Dumpster. As soon as she had the photo, she forwarded it, along with the license plate number, to Lee Carrington's cell phone, asking via text message, *Lee, is this one of ours? Jacey.* Finally, she heard the Ford retreat, turn around and head back up Mesa Street towards Moraga Avenue.

Cautiously, Jacey waited another ten minutes. Lee's answer came back in the interim, *Will check it out.* Then, Jacey proceeded through the alleys toward her father's condo, increasingly aware of the darkness settling on the neighborhood. Finally, she slipped through the condo's back entrance when she thought it was safe to do so.

"Hi!" exclaimed Jake. "Did I lock the front door?"

"No," she responded, hoping her voice sounded casual. "I jogged a different route home, is all. A little change of scenery is always good, don't you think? It's getting dark earlier these days, isn't it?" She put the bag on the counter and went into her bedroom without another word. Her bedroom window opened onto Moraga Avenue, and she cautiously stood to the side, looking out nervously through the thin curtains. The black Ford Explorer was parked across the street several buildings away. With the darkness encroaching, Jacey knew she had to act quickly. She changed into a pair of dark jeans and a black sweater.

It was time to get her father out of danger. She stepped into the bathroom and turned on the shower to mask the noise of her call, then she pressed a button on speed dial. The call was answered, "Director of Operations, what is your emergency?"

"This is SF 92791, reporting a foreign shadow outside my father's condominium on Moraga."

"One moment, please. I'll connect you."

Jacey only had to wait a few seconds, but it seemed much longer. When she heard Lee Carrington's voice, she felt absolute relief. "Agent Munroe, the Explorer was purchased from a rental agency two days ago. They don't seem to have a name on the driver. Oh, wait! Here it comes. John Smith. Original. And, because it was purchased and not rented, they won't have a driver's license. Address is . . . in the middle of San Francisco Bay. Entirely useless. The point being, it isn't one of ours, and that means you and your father are no longer safe. Can you make it to Sheridan and Lincoln without being seen?"

"Yes. We'll take the alleys," she whispered.

"I'll have someone there shortly."

The line went dead. Leaving the shower running, Jacey went back into her bedroom and reached into the closet where she unlocked a small safe she had hidden behind her clothes. Taking out a belt holding a holster, handgun and extra ammo clips, Jacey slipped it around her waist and pulled her sweater over it.

Retreating to the kitchen, she noticed her father had already started mixing the cookie dough. "Mmm, Dad, that's very thoughtful, thanks." She turned the kitchen faucet on full blast and turned up the volume on the radio.

"What is it?" her father asked, the color blanching from his face.

"We have to go right now, Dad," she answered. "Put on your darkest jacket."

Jake's eyes widened in alarm. "It'll take me all of three seconds."

"Hurry," she said, removing her Glock 27 from its holster. "I'll watch the front. When you're at the back door, ring the doorbell, will you? Maybe they'll think the noise is coming from another part of the building." She stepped into the living room, standing away from the front window, but close enough to look out. Although night had drenched the city in blackness, street lights flooded neighboring buildings. The Ford remained parked up the street, but two men in dark clothing were getting out of the Explorer. They headed toward her condo.

Jake and Jacey would have to travel on foot because both their cars were parked in the front of the condo. It was too risky to try and sneak around to the front, it would expose her father to danger, which she would not do. Jacey knew the people in the Ford had waited for complete darkness for only one reason. They did not want to be seen.

As the back doorbell rang, Jacey dashed out and found that her father had put on a charcoal jacket, and had their passports and a handful of cash. "I doubt we'll need that, Dad, but maybe. You never know. We're heading for the corner of Lincoln and Sheridan. Stay in the shadows, move quietly, quickly, and don't look back for me. Just go."

She slid the door shut and waited just a second or two to see her father head up the alley. Suddenly, the front door of her condo burst open and gunfire sprayed the living room and kitchen. Jacey raced to catch up to Jake. "Behind that car, Dad. Hurry," she whispered, jumping up and sliding over the hood of an old Buick where she landed on the other side. "Hunch down by the tire, Dad, so they can't see your feet."

Her father crouched down into position, following her instructions.

A few more bursts of gunfire, rapid-repeaters, blasted the once quiet neighborhood, then the back door to their apartment flew open and a man came into the alley. Another man, apparently from inside the apartment, yelled, "Anything?"

The man in the alley barked, "No, they're long gone. Let's get out of here before the cops show up."

When they left, Jake said, "Call the police on your cell, Jacey."

"No, Dad. We take our orders only from the FBI."

"We should at least take one of the cars," he persisted.

"No. Those men could have left someone behind to watch the cars, or they could have planted them with explosives or monitors. Come on, let's go to our rendezvous point."

"Out of the shadows, quietly and quickly, isn't that what you said?" he asked with a grimace.

Jacey nodded. "Let's go!"

They ran most of the way, staying in the alleys and deserted side streets, away from street lamps and well-lit buildings. Zigging and zagging a trail down alleys from Moraga to Sheridan, Jacey and Jake avoided sirens racing up Mesa toward their condo. Soon, they were spotted by Federal agents in a gray service van. They were picked up and taken to the FBI's San Francisco office, where they were led downstairs to a planning room.

Lee Carrington, Agent Hill and several other agents were deep in discussion when Jacey and

Jake arrived. Lee shook their hands. "Agent Munroe, Dr. Munroe, glad you were able to get out. The police have swarmed over your place, but they haven't seen the Explorer yet. We've got an all-points bulletin out on it."

"How did they find me?" she asked.

"We don't know," Lee said. "But, Katie is scheduled to testify against her father on Monday, so we expected Myles Chester to turn up the heat."

"What can I do to help?" Jacey asked.

Agent Hill shook his head, "Nothing. The Chester woman is in a safe-house in Washington, D.C., until Monday."

Jacey went ballistic with his nonchalant attitude. "If they can find me, they can find her. We're not doing enough!"

"Calm down," said Lee. "What do you suggest?"

Jacey didn't have to think about it for long. "We should bring Katie into the Justice Department building tonight and keep her secluded under heavy guard. Then, assign me to take Katie's place at the safe-house. This way, no one but an insider will know which of us is the real Katie Chester. If we don't do more than we're doing, you can kiss Katie's testimony goodbye," advised Jacey.

"Isn't that a little overkill?" snarled Agent Hill.

"I'd also suggest you remove anyone with that kind of mentality from the case," Jacey said to Lee as she glared at Agent Hill. "When you've walked in Katie Chester's shoes, Agent Hill, you might have a clue as to how desperate her father is to prevent her from testifying."

"No disrespect intended, Agent Munroe," said Agent Hill, but his scowl indicated otherwise.

Lee Carrington interrupted them. "This agency has spent several million dollars trying to bring Chester down. We're well aware of his propensity for violence."

"Wait," said Special Agent Connelly as he walked into the room. "Agent Munroe's suggestion has merit." Apparently, he had been listening in behind a mirrored wall. "We have rooms within the Department of Justice in Washington, D.C., where we could guard Ms. Chester, get her completely off the streets until the day of her testimony. I agree with Agent Munroe. She could replace her at the safe-house, acting as a decoy. I doubt that Myles Chester has the manpower to go after two targets at once. Word on the street is he's hurting financially since we froze his assets. And, we've eliminated most of his thugs."

"It's a waste of resources," grumbled Agent Hill, "but since I'm not calling the shots, do as you see fit."

Special Agent Connelly seemed to be mulling the situation over in his mind. "We don't seem able to prevent Chester from finding Agent Munroe. Her life's in danger no matter where we task her."

"Fine," she said, "but get me a wig this time. I'm not dying my hair again."

Connelly almost laughed.

"And one more thing," suggested Jacey. "My father stays here under protective custody. Assign someone to watch him twenty-four-seven until this thing is over. Once Katie Chester has testified, we'll all rest easy."

"Done," agreed Connelly.

"Jacey, I'm going with you," persuaded Jake.

Looking him squarely in the face, she said, "No, Dad. You need to stay here. Who's going to tell the FBI what color to paint the condo when they remove all the bullets?"

Her father almost smiled. "That's unimportant right now. I need to go with you."

"You can't. This isn't your battle, Dad. It's mine."

"It's too dangerous," he insisted.

"It's who I am," she answered. "It's all those many reasons you love me. Let the ice cream spill where it does, Dad. You can wash your hair later."

He gulped and she saw the recognition in his eyes as he realized she had to do this on her own. "All right," he finally answered. "But, this time come back in one piece."

Chapter Thirteen

In Washington, D.C., the following morning, Jacey and Lee met with Director Stevens, Special Agent Connelly, and a dozen other agents gathered together in one large room on the third floor of the Department of Justice. They were divided up into two nine-person teams, one team assigned to Jacey, who was disguised as Katie Chester, and one team guarding the real Katie Chester.

Lee Carrington's team, which included Connelly and Hill, would be guarding the real Katie Chester. Jacey was to be secreted into the same safe-house where Katie had been hiding up until last night, when she was moved under cover of darkness to a heavily guarded room somewhere inside the massive Department of Justice building. After both groups had been assigned their missions, they were dismissed to go to their posts. Jacey was assigned to Agent Johnson's team. The safe-house where Katie Chester had been kept until late last night was nothing more than an abandoned house in a run-down neighborhood north of Washington, D.C. Jacey and the rest of the team would have to wait thirty-six hours until Katie Chester was scheduled to testify.

Jacey immediately considered it prudent to wear her wig and contact lenses. If they were ambushed early on, whoever did the ambushing might think they'd made a good hit, considering how closely Jacey resembled Katie Chester.

The agents took turns sleeping four hours on, four hours off, until it would be time to move their decoy. Jacey found sleep a fleeting thing. Exhaustion wore on her, but around midnight Sunday night, she finally fell asleep.

At three in the morning, Jacey was awakened by Lee Carrington. She sat upright, coming to full attention. "Why aren't you at the Department of Justice?" she asked.

"Shh," Lee whispered. "Give me five minutes lead, then meet me in the bathroom."

Jacey nodded and stretched back out on her cot, pretending to be asleep. In her mind, she counted out the seconds, giving Lee the time he needed to rendezvous with her. In the back of her mind, she wondered just how safe a safe-house could be if Lee had slipped in undetected by the men supposedly guarding her. When five minutes passed, she got up, pretended to stumble around sleepily, then headed toward the bathroom, making certain the field agents on duty knew that was where she was going.

When Jacey closed the bathroom door, she was surprised to see Lee helping a woman into the bathroom through a window. Maintaining her silence, Jacey waited patiently, noting the woman's red hair and green eyes, but no other resemblance to Katie Chester. Jacey whispered, "What's this all about?"

"She's your replacement," said Lee. "Borrowed her from the Bureau. Katie Chester, meet Katie Chester."

The woman nodded, then she and Jacey exchanged clothing . When they had finished, the woman asked,"Where should I go?"

"Second door on the right, down the hall," said Jacey. After she left quietly, Jacey turned to Lee. "What's going on?"

"I have orders to take you to Director Stevens, ASAP." He nodded toward the window. "Need a hand up?"

Jacey shook her head.

Lee warned, "Stay to the left of the window, as close to the wall as you can. I'll direct you through the camera shadows once I join you."

"See you outside," said Jacey as she pulled herself up to the window and scooted her way out, then dropped to the ground about eight feet below. When Lee arrived, Jacey followed in his footsteps as they hid in the shadows of trees and hedges, then made their way up the street to a limousine. Quickly, they entered one of the back doors and the limousine whisked towards the city.

After ten minutes of corner turning and alley driving, the car turned onto a highway and finally kept to one lane, going with the flow of sparse traffic. "Sorry about that," said the driver, and Jacey recognized the voice immediately.

"Director Stevens?" she asked in surprise.

He nodded. "Agent Munroe, you hit the nail on the head in San Francisco. We haven't been able to protect you during this assignment, and I fear we have a mole amongst us. I am most reluctant to put you in harm's way again, but as you are the closest in resemblance, I wonder if you would take Ms. Chester's place until the trial?"

"I'd be honored, sir," Jacey responded.

"No one will know of this switch in plans but the five of us," continued Director Stevens.

"Yourself, Agent Carrington, Ms. Chester and her decoy, and me. We've got to flush this fellow out if Ms. Chester is ever to live long enough to testify. And, I think we can say the same for you."

"I agree. What plans have you made?" she asked.

"I'm afraid at this late date, my plans are not as elaborate as you might hope. You and Agent Carrington will have to improvise as you go along. I've briefed him as much as I can on such short notice."

"We improvise nicely when we have to," Jacey said as a sick feeling started to well up in her stomach. Fortunately, her adrenalin also started pumping, which seemed to ease her fear.

"You'll find blueprints of the Department of Justice and some appropriate clothing on the front seat. I will be entering the garage in precisely twenty-seven minutes. I suggest you stay alert." He slammed on the brakes.

The car came to a screeching halt. Director Stevens got out, stepped two or three feet away, climbed into the back of a second limousine that drove away, leaving Lee and Jacey completely on their own. Scrambling over the front seat, Jacey said, "I'll read the blueprints. You drive."

Lee climbed into the front seat after her. "Worried?" he asked.

"Exactly," she answered.

Turning on a small dash light so she could study the blueprints of the building, Jacey said, "I don't see any way in except the normal entrances."

"The parking garage," said Lee. "The director gave us that one."

Jacey nodded and proceeded to study the garage. "There's a service elevator at the rear, an air duct can be accessed three floors up. Three junctions later I could drop down one level to the second floor, and go due east until I'm directly over the room where Katie Chester is being held."

"How do you know where we're keeping her?" Lee asked, turning a sharp corner.

Removing a yellow piece of paper from the blueprint, she said, "Director Stevens left me a note." Jacey grinned at him mischievously.

Lee smiled. "I'll help you when I'm on duty. I'm scheduled at six a.m."

"So, everyone thinks you're asleep?" she asked.

"No, they think I'm in the conference room with Director Stevens."

"If all goes well, I should be able to join you shortly," said Jacey as she pulled on the long-sleeved, black jumpsuit left for her by Director Stevens, and noticed there were rubber patches on the knees and elbows. "Whatever do you suppose these are for?" Jacey asked.

"I suppose to prevent you from slipping down one of the vertical ducts," Lee said, following another limousine in through the open garage doors. "I'll swing by the rear elevator, and you'll get out on a slowing turn. Do you think you can do that?"

"I've gotten into a moving helicopter before, I think I can manage it," affirmed Jacey.

"To starboard, then," he said. "On three." Lee started to make a turn around the center aisle at the end of the garages. "One. Two."

Jacey didn't hear the three. She was out of the door, running along side the limousine in a hunching manner until she reached the elevator, pressed the "up" button and sank into a shadow until the door opened. Dashing inside, she pressed the number three and waited for the elevator to ascend. It didn't take long. She hit the "stop" button between two and three, pressed the door open, and used the floor from three, which was now waist level, to wedge her way up through the elevator's ceiling hatch. Then, she looked around to see where the air duct might be located.

A sudden lurch almost threw her off the elevator roof as it started moving upward, right past the air duct opening. After several stops later, up and down, the elevator finally started down again, toward the bottom of the building. Jacey watched carefully until the elevator whisked to level four, guessed where the air duct opening would be, and threw herself into it as the elevator zoomed by.

Clank. Clank. Clunk. It could have been quieter, but she didn't know that she had a choice. Arriving a little bruised, but apparently unbroken, she slithered along the duct, over three open parallel ducts, then started her descent to the second floor.

To her dismay, she found more dust and cobwebs inside the duct than she had imagined possible. Inching her way in what she thought was an easterly direction above the second floor, she undulated over an empty court room and two smaller rooms before she found the windowless room where Katie Chester was waiting until her turn to testify at her father's trial.

Within the room, Jacey saw a porta-potty, a portable sink, a waste basket, a small refrigerator, a table, two chairs and a cot made up for sleeping. A pitcher of water, a half-crumpled bag of chips, a deck of cards and an empty glass stood on the table. Katie Chester was pacing back and forth like a caged animal. Indeed, that was what she had become. It sickened Jacey to see it. At least when Jacey was secluded at the Crow's Nest, she had the hallways and stairs to run up and down. Here, Katie had nothing but the four walls closing in on her.

Lee arrived shortly after Jacey reached the airspace over the heavily-guarded room. He made his presence known by knocking at the door.

"Come in," said Katie, turning to face him.

Opening the door, Lee said, "Good morning, Ms. Chester. I'm Agent Carrington, and I will be leading the team guarding you from now through the trial. Is there anything I can get for you?"

Katie shook her head, then implored. "Aren't you the agent I sat next to on the plane from New York to Edinburgh?"

"Yes, Ma'am," Lee said.

"Well, sit yourself down and play a game of fish with me, darling," she said. "I'm bored with solitaire. They won't let me have a television set or a radio. They don't want me to hear anything from the trial, you know. And the country tunes they downloaded to this I-pod are so lame."

"I can't," said Lee, closing the door behind him.

"Spoil sport," she teased.

"No, Ma'am," Lee argued. "But, I am here to inform you that an executive decision has been made, and I have to move you one more time before the trial. And, if you think this room has been hard to live in, you should see where I'm planning to put you next."

"Don't tell me, some tiny lavatory?" she asked, apparently dismayed at this news.

"No, it's even worse than that," said Lee. "Agent Munroe, now would be a good time."

Jacey sighed in relief and lifted the grate on the air duct. Katie nearly screamed, but Lee put his hand over her mouth just in time.

Lowering herself into the room wasn't too difficult once Lee moved the table into the middle of the room. When Jacey reached the floor, she brushed off some of the dust and cobwebs, then looked into the surprised eyes of Katie Chester. "Good morning, Katie. I'm sorry I frightened you."

"Genius!" exclaimed Katie. "It's you again." Then, as she realized what was next, she said, "You surely don't think I'm going to go up in that air duct, do you? Look at yourself, Agent . . . why, I don't even know your name."

"Jacey Munroe," said Jacey, shaking her hand.

"You're covered in cobwebs and dust and heaven only knows what else!" gasped Katie.

"It may be the only way we can save your life," explained Jacey.

"I am not going up in that ceiling, I don't care what you say!" Katie exploded.

"Believe me, Katie, you are going up in that hole, and you're not going to complain about it," insisted Jacey. "You're going up in that hole for me."

"Give me one reason why I should," demanded Katie.

Jacey quelled her temper, but she was certain some of it showed through when she hissed, ". . . I've been shot, shot at, abducted, kidnapped, my pilot was poisoned in order to crash my airplane, I had to smash up a BMW protecting your life, I went sailing off a bridge and was dumped into the River Tweed, and I nearly drowned for you."

"But, that's your job, Agent Munroe," Katie whimpered.

"Remember what I said to you on the plane?" Jacey asked. "Do you really want to put your father behind bars or do you want to become another of his victims?"

"I will testify, Agent Munroe. I just don't want to go up in that hole up there," she whined.

Jacey shook your head and shrugged. "Okay, forget it, Lee. I'll meet you back out at the car. There is one good thing about Katie and me being such a close match. We'll know what size to order her coffin."

She climbed back up on the table, but Katie grabbed her pant leg and said, "You're not going to protect me anymore?"

"Not unless you're willing to put yourself in an uncomfortable spot for about three hours," Jacey insisted.

Jacey could see the debate going through Katie's mind and persuaded, "Katie, someone in the agency is in your dad's pocket. He's been one step ahead of us since I left Forbes Manor at Galashiels. If we don't exchange places, you will probably be dead within the next three hours."

Katie's mouth dropped open and she started to shake. "Will you put a blanket down, first? I hate dust and cobwebs and . . . what is that thing in your hair?"

Jacey whipped off her wig and shook it. A small spider landed on the floor and Lee promptly stepped on it.

"There," Lee said with a smile. "Agent Munroe swept the spiders out for you."

Katie shivered. "I want all my bedding and my pillow up there, too. And, I want a flashlight in case someone turns out the light."

"Done," said Lee. "Why don't you ladies change clothes and switch places while I round up a flashlight?" Lee slipped out the door and Jacey locked it behind him.

It took some doing, but Jacey soon changed clothing with Katie, helped the poor woman up into the air duct with her pillow and blanket and bed sheets, then spent some time cleaning the cobwebs out of her wig and making sure there were no more spiders prepared to set up house within its red curly locks. After scrubbing her face, Jacey put on some of Katie's makeup.

By the time Lee got back, ninety minutes had passed. Jacey knew it was daylight outside, it was already seven-thirty in the morning, but because the room was windowless, she couldn't tell if it was raining, snowing or clear. Jacey tossed a bag of breakfast Lee had purchased, along with a flashlight, up to Katie, waited for her to replace the grate, then sat at the table silently to listen for any sounds that might indicate trouble.

At twenty after eight, Katie had to climb down to go to the bathroom, and gloated that she hadn't encountered a single spider so far.

After helping Katie back into the air duct ten minutes later, Jacey counted off the seconds until the guards would escort her to the courtroom. Grateful Lee would be among them, Jacey removed her Glock 27 from her waist holster and checked that it was fully loaded, including a bullet in the chamber. Snugly, she pulled the belts on her bullet-proof vest, and returned the handgun to its holster.

Finally, at ten minutes to nine, Katie heard an armed escort arriving for her, and knew they would open the door just as soon as they ascertained that the halls were cleared. "Now, remember," she whispered up to Katie. "It doesn't matter what you hear, don't come down from there until Lee or I bring you down."

"What if you both get shot or something?" Katie intoned.

"Then, don't come down unless Director Stevens is present," Jacey insisted.

"Did you really get shot?" Katie asked.

"Yes, and much, much worse," said Jacey.

"I'm sorry you had to go through all that," said Katie. "My father . . . I used to respect him, but not since . . . well, I know what I have to do. Good luck, Jacey."

"Just tell the jurors the truth and everything will work out," promised Jacey.

A knock came at the door. "Who is it?" Jacey asked.

"Agent Carrington, ready to move you to the courtroom, Ma'am," said Lee.

"Come in," said Jacey. "I'm ready." This time she tried to make her voice sound like Katie's nasally twang.

The door swung open, and Jacey made eye contact only with Lee Carrington. Otherwise, she kept her head down, as though fearful of everyone. Lee was accompanied by eight other men heavily armed, bullet-proof gear on their chests, heads, arms, and thighs, with weapons ready.

"This way, Ma'am," said Lee, putting her right in the center of them. "Just as I instructed."

They started to move forward up the hall. Suddenly, Jacey felt an urgent need to trust her instincts and she turned around to walk backwards. The man who planned to kill her would probably not be walking in front of her, he would be walking behind her. She saw a flash of silver, a hand out of place, and she twisted her body out of its mark just in time to avoid being stabbed. As the hand came inside her circle to try again, she grabbed the man's wrist and twisted it for all she was worth. The other guards barely had time to react. To her astonishment, it was Agent Hill who broke her grip, pulled her up against him and placed the knife blade at her neck. Lee pointed the barrel of his rifle at Agent Hill's temple, as did seven other agents.

"It was you!" Jacey gasped. "It was you all along?"

Hill reacted the moment he recognized her voice. His brief hesitation gave Jacey the split-second she needed. In one swift motion, she bit his hand with all her strength and slammed him against the wall, then twisted herself out of his grasp. He screamed out in pain as he dropped the knife. Realizing he could not escape, he held his hands in the air.

Immediately, Lee turned Agent Hill against the wall and put him in handcuffs.

"Good job, Agent Munroe. You got him," said Director Stevens as he headed toward them from another room, bringing five more guards and Special Agent Connelly with him. "Take Mr. Hill down to the holding cell," he directed.

"Why wasn't I told about this change of plans?" demanded Special Agent Connelly.

"Process of elimination," said Director Stevens. "I didn't know who might be the mole."

Jacey was shaking so much she thought her knees would buckle, but then she remembered

Katie Chester. "Let's get the real witness into the courtroom," she said with a smile, surprised at how steady her voice sounded against the pounding of adrenalin through her veins.

Chapter Fourteen

Back in San Francisco, Jacey listened to the evening news with her father as they hung the last of the ornaments on their Christmas tree. The condo had been completely plastered and painted in her absence. New carpet and kitchen cupboards and appliances had been installed and the furniture replaced. Still, it was home to her, and home meant holiday decorations.

The newscaster said, "Former billionaire, Myles Chester, made headline news today when the jury came back this morning with a guilty verdict on all charges. While the prosecution is seeking the death penalty, defense attorneys are expected to argue for a lighter sentence. Sentencing deliberations are set to begin on Monday. Katie Chester, who testified against her father last month, could not be located for comment, but sources close to the family say half of the Chester empire still belongs to Ms. Chester, since it was bequeathed in her mother's will several years ago. The Justice Department has seized control of all the remaining Chester holdings and bank accounts. "

"You did it, Agent Jacey Munroe," said Jake proudly. "You saved a woman's life and got a scoundrel off the streets forever."

"Provided he doesn't have more people on the outside who want to finish his dirty work," Jacey said. "Myles Chester is evil incarnate. I've been worried he'll still make trouble for Katie once he's incarcerated."

"He can't," Jake insisted philosophically. "Chester doesn't have enough money left to hire a bodyguard for himself while in prison. And, where he's going, he'll need one."

When the telephone rang, Jacey picked up the receiver and answered, "Hello."

"Jacey?" came an anxious male voice. She recognized it immediately.

"Rob? Rob, is that you?" she asked as tears welled up in her eyes.

"Aye, lass, 'tis me," he answered.

Jacey had never heard a Scottish accent that sounded so welcome before. "How did you–"

"Have I waited long enough, Jacey?" he asked, interrupting her. "I do not want to risk bringing any harm to ye. 'Tis why I have remained silent all these weeks, waiting for the trial to end."

"No," she gasped. "Oh, no, Rob, it's never too late."

"May I see you, lass?" The ragged inflection of his voice indicated how much he had missed her. Jacey was thrilled to hear it.

"Yes, yes, of course," she answered.

"When?" he asked. "Tonight?"

"Rob, I'm in San Francisco," she said, not considering since he had telephoned her, he very likely knew where she lived.

He laughed aloud. "Aye, lass. As am I."

"You are?" Jacey did not understand.

"Yes. Shall I come over right away?"

"No, I'll– " she didn't want Rob to meet her father just yet. She and Rob still had so much to sort out. "Do you know where Long Avenue turns onto Marine Drive?"

"Aye, I've been there many times."

"I'll meet you at . . . *The End of the Road*," she said, hoping he understood what she meant.

"I'll be there in thirty minutes," Rob responded.

The line went dead before she could say anymore. Jacey looked at her father. "It's Rob," she told him, answering the puzzled expression on Jake's face. "I don't know how he did it, but somehow he found me."

"How does your heart feel about that?" Jake asked her.

"It's– it's singing," she intoned. "You were right, Dad. Love grows stronger every moment."

"Do you want me to drive you over there?" he asked.

"No offense, Dad, but I think we need some time alone," she said, not wanting to hurt her father's feelings.

He stood and gave her a fatherly hug. "I understand, Jacey. It's your time for love, and you must go wherever it takes you."

" I must look terrible," she said as she kissed Jake's cheek. She dashed into the bathroom, freshened her makeup and ran a brush through her golden brown hair until it sparkled. Then, slipping into a light mint-colored dress, she wrapped herself in a warm sweater, put on a matching pair of heels and grabbed an umbrella, remembering the weatherman had predicted rain.

"You won't be needing this?" her father asked, holding up her holster and handgun.

Jacey laughed. "No, I don't believe those will help me at all tonight, Dad."

Within minutes, Jacey was driving down Marine Drive toward the Golden Gate Bridge. The parking lot at the end of Marine Drive was completely deserted this time of night, probably because the malls were filled with holiday shoppers. Turning the car into a vacant parking space, she set the brake and turned the engine off.

Within moments, a taxicab pulled up and a man got out of the back, handing some cash to the driver. Jacey would have recognized Robert Roy McLennan anywhere, but here in the dense fog, he seemed even more remarkable.

Jacey flashed her headlights once, then got out of the car and shut the door. Then, Jacey stood her ground. Watching Rob walk through the mist toward her was like watching an angel arrive straight out of heaven. Still, she waited.

When Rob was within three feet of her, Jacey could restrain herself no longer. She crossed the space and threw herself into his open arms, kissing his cheeks, his neck, his lips again and again, laughing and crying at the same time.

"Oh, Rob," she wept. "I've missed you so. I love you so."

"Aye, and I feel the same, lass, as ye plainly know," he said, kissing her all the more.

A thundercloud boomed ominously overhead, but she didn't care if the rain would soon drive them to seek shelter inside the car.

When she finally stopped crying, and they had confessed their love for one another a dozen times, Jacey whispered, "I can't believe you're really here."

"Where did ye expect me to be, lass? Sitting in Galashiels, while the woman I love is pining for me in San Francisco?" A teasing smile widened his mouth and sank dimples into his cheeks.

"How did you find me?" she wondered.

"Ye asked me to find ye," he answered, apparently surprised that she did not know. "It wasn't too difficult to find a Jake Munroe working in a Physical Therapy Center in San Francisco. He's listed in the phone book, lass. Surely ye knew that when ye sent the letter to me."

Confused, Jacey said, "But, I never sent you a letter, Rob. I swear. I wrote one, but I destroyed it."

"No," he confessed. "It arrived on my doorstep over a month ago. I flew directly to San Francisco when I received it, and have been staying at the Marriott ever since, waiting for Myles Chester's trial to end. When I heard the news tonight on the television, I hoped it would not be endangering your life to finally call ye."

"That's impossible," Jacey shook her head. "I wrote a letter to you while Dad and I were in San Diego, but I torched it in the gas grill that same night."

"This letter?" he asked, pulling three pieces of stationary from his pocket and giving them to her.

Jacey could not see the writing in the dark. Rob pulled a penlight from his pocket and shone it upon the paper. It was her letter, that much was certain, for her handwriting was plainly discernible. But the ink looked the color of burnt umber, and the edges of the stationery were seared.

"I don't understand," she said. "I burned all three pages in the gas grill at the condo where we were staying."

"That would explain why it arrived without an envelope," he said huskily.

"My mother!" she gasped. "I've felt for a long time that she's been watching over me, ever since she died."

"Then, this letter is proof positive that the Scottish Legend has ended."

Jacey whispered, "I didn't really understand what Rachel told me about the legend, but she also told me you couldn't father children."

"Yet, ye are willing to marry me anyway?" he asked.

To answer him, Jacey kissed him passionately. When she let him up for air, she said, "We can adopt if we choose. Oh, Rob, I cannot tell you how terrible these past few months have been without you."

"Nor I, ye," he said thoughtfully. "But, before I propose, Miss Munroe, I must ask ye two questions."

Rob's voice changed to complete seriousness, and Jacey gave him her undivided attention. "What?" she asked. "My answer is yes to both of them."

"Did ye know that the Scottish Legend began when a McLennan clansman fell in love with a Munroe, but his parents refused them permission to marry?"

Jacey's eyes widened in surprise. "A Munroe?" she questioned. "Rachel didn't tell me the other clan's name."

"No McLennan has ever been happy in love since that time. 'Twas told until a McLennan and a Munroe marry, the unhappiness would continue forever. Perhaps, 'twas your mother who left the letter upon my doorstep, lass."

Smiling, Jacey said, "That answers one of the questions, what is the other?"

"Do ye want to have children, Jacey? Children from ye and me?"

Trick question, thought Jacey. She did not have an immediate answer, so she trusted her instincts. "I want whatever is best for us, Rob, and only God knows the answer to that."

"Then I may as well confess," Rob responded. "'Tis true my first wife left me when I told her I could not father children."

"I know," Jacey began, but he placed his fingers upon her lips to hush her.

"I told her I could not father children," he confessed. "But, the truth is, I found out after we married she was only after my money. Scottish laws would have guaranteed her a lifelong income if we'd had a child. I want my children to have a mother who loves them because they are an intimate part of her and me, not for what riches she may acquire by having them."

"You lied?" she asked in amazement.

"It seemed the simplest way to protect my future children, lass. Does it disturb ye to know the truth about me?" He gave her an awkward smile.

"You had to wade through my lies to get to the truth, and you stayed the course. I think, Mr. McLennan, that I can do the same." Jacey put her hands upon his shoulders and thrilled as he pulled her close and kissed her so thoroughly she could never doubt the depth or intensity of their love.

A gentle rain started out as a sprinkle, and soon turned into a downpour, but the two lovers were inseparable. Finally, the weather won out, and they sought safe shelter from the storm inside Jacey's car.

"Miss Munroe," said Rob quickly between kisses. "Shall we marry before our ancestors learn we have? I wouldn't want the McLennans handing out some belated form of retribution."

"Straight away," she agreed, loving the Scottish Legend who held her in his arms and promised to make the world right for her . . . ever after.

Epilogue:

From a cozy recliner in their living room, Jacey had just finished nursing her six-month old son, Jacob Robert McLennan, where mother and child were still snuggling. The late news had ended, and her sleepy family was about to retire for the night when the telephone rang.

Rob automatically handed the receiver to Jacey, having learned early on in their marriage that ninety percent of the calls were for his wife.

"Hello," Jacey mumbled, trying to keep her eyes open.

"Mrs. McLennan, we need you to fly from Edinburgh to Paris on the morning of December 22nd at 10:15 A.M."

"No," she said, wondering why December 22nd seemed so familiar to her. Did she already have an appointment that day? "I haven't been flying for the Bureau for over a year. I only serve part-time as a field agent out of the Scotland offices. And, my flight time is only for fun these days."

She heard a familiar laugh, and realized her caller was Lee Carrington. "Lee," she grinned. "I haven't heard from you for ages. How are you?"

"You talk to my wife, Rachel, all the time," he complained. "Why don't you ever call me?"

"Rachel keeps me up to date on how your marriage is working," she teased. To Rob, she said, "Please put on the speaker phone for me, sweetheart."

Rob pressed a button and hung up the handset for her, then turned off the television. "You may as well know," came Lee's forlorn voice from the speaker phone. "I'm in terrible trouble."

"Why? What's wrong?" Jacey asked.

"Rachel says she doesn't want me for her birthing coach."

"Why not?" Jacey didn't understand.

Lee explained, "She wants someone with a little more experience. Will you come?"

"Of course, I'll be her birthing coach, but why is she having the baby in December . . . I thought she wasn't due until spring?" asked Jacey, confused.

"She's due in March," came his cagey response.

Rob nibbled at Jacey's ear with his warm lips, making her want to put the baby in his crib and take her husband to bed with her. Instead, she tucked her ear against her shoulder and asked Lee, "Then, what's happening in Paris?"

"I promised Katie Chester I'd get you there for her Christmas wedding. She wants you to cover the security aspect."

Jacey reacted immediately. "If you think for one minute I'm going to walk down the aisle with another man–" Jacey began, but Rob shushed her with his fingers on her lips.

"Ye are sadly mistaken," Rob finished the sentence for her. "Not my wife! And, that's my final answer."

Kneeling in front of Jacey, Rob caressed young Jacob's face. Their son crinkled his nose and pushed his father's hand away, but remained sound asleep.

"I don't think you understand the enormity of the situation," came Lee's voice from the speaker phone. "She wants a big wedding, and that means publicity. She needs someone to double for her . . ."

Jacey and Rob ignored Lee's voice completely.

Nodding to Rob to take their son, she hoped Jacob would stay asleep this time. They had already put him to bed twice that night.

Rob lifted their son into his strong arms and carried him upstairs to the nursery, with Jacey following close behind them. She watched with secret delight as Rob lovingly kissed Jacob's forehead, placed Jacob in his crib, then covered him with a cozy blanket.

Jacey reached out and stroked Jacob's brown, curly locks. Her infant son rolled onto his side, away from her. He gave a little sigh and slept peacefully.

Smiling, Rob pulled Jacey into his arms and kissed her hungrily. He took her hand and led her into the master bedroom, closing the door behind them.

Downstairs, the speaker phone announced Lee Carrington's continuous protestations. But, Rob and Jacey gave up listening long ago.

<u>Introducing Sherry Ann Miller's five-book *Gift Series*</u>

If you enjoyed reading **Scottish Legend**, you're going to love all five novels in Sherry Ann Miller's popular *Gift Series*, which can be read out of sequence without losing continuity. The *Gift Series* will take you on the individual sojourns of Kayla Dawn Allen and the five men who have influenced her life for good: the Sparkleman boys, Ed, Abbot and Tom, who grew up with Kayla on the *Bar M Ranch*; and the sea-faring Clark twins, Joshua (who loves Kayla more than life itself) and Hans (who is always one step behind in finding his soul-mate). Each novel will plunge you into a miraculous, spine-tingling journey about life, love, heartache and triumphant joy. If you've a thirst for suck-you-in adventure, drama, action and romance, you'll want to read all five novels in Sherry Ann's award-winning *Gift Series:*

One Last Gift

Lovely Kayla is rescued from her own scientific disposition, her misguided infatuation with Ed Sparkleman, and even more desperate and dangerous elements in *One Last Gift.*

Kayla's remarkable journey from her sailboat in San Diego to her childhood home high in the Uinta Mountains, finds her facing one obstacle after another, until she finally discovers God's mighty miracles are all around her. At the miraculous and satisfying conclusion, you will be left with the question, "What about Ed?"

An Angel's Gift

Ed Sparkleman meets his match when Alyssa drops in on the *Bar M Ranch* (literally!) and disrupts his life forever. As ranch foreman, Ed is responsible for keeping his men in order, but with Alyssa around, all the ranch hands begin to act oddly out of character . . .especially Ed. Is Alyssa truly *An Angel's Gift* sent straight to him from heaven? If so, what about his brother, Abbot?

The Tyee's Gift

Set in the picturesque Pacific Northwest, adventure meets Abbot Sparkleman when he discovers the greatest archaeological site of the century and falls in love with the beautiful and mysterious Bekah. *The Tyee's Gift* will bring tears of laughter, joy and heartache while Abbot learns where much is given, much is required.

Charity's Gift

When Hans comes face to face with a ferocious shark, it strikes less fear than vivacious
and attractive Charity, who throws his heart into
a spiraling nose-dive deep in the Pacific Ocean.
The only way he can salvage their crumbling
romance is to find her missing father, who's
been absent from Charity's life for more than
twenty years. *Charity's Gift* will touch your
heart forever.

The Refiner's Gift   Coming Soon!

The fifth and final novel in the *Gift Series* is now in progress, and answers the wor-
risome question, "What about Tom?" who was
accused of a vicious crime in *One Last Gift*,
six years ago. Tom Sparkleman has not yet escaped the consequences of that crime. The
miracle that awaits him in *The Refiner's Gift*
will astound everyone.

* * * * *

<u>Sherry Ann Miller's two-book</u> <u>*Warwick Saga*</u>

Historical fiction at its very best!

Search for the Bark Warwick

Beginning with the stowaway who interrupts and changes John's life forever, and concluding with John's desperate search for his captive son, this historical novel, based loosely on a true story, is a stirring tale of surprise, compassion, love and tenacious devotion to family. The story of a genuine hero in 1630's England, *Search for the Bark Warwick* will keep you on the edge of your seat, and leave you begging for more.

Search for the Warwick II

Proving once and for all why she is known as the writer of miracles, Sherry Ann Miller's absorbing sequel, *Search for the Warwick II*, concludes the search for John Dunton's son who is enslaved in 1630's Algeria, where a generous reward has been offered for John's capture. Now, John must not only find Thomas, he must avoid recapture while he and his devoted crew attempt to outsail and outmaneuver a horde of evil pirates. Nothing else matters to John or his men . . . not even their own lives.

The Warwick Saga is complete in two novels and should be read in sequence.

* * * * *

And don't miss . . .

Oregon Flame:

Nicole Travis could easily fall for Wade Reilly's fiery charm, if only she could trust him. But, how can Nicole ever believe Wade's sincerity? He took advantage of her brother, and destroyed her relationship with her fiancé. ***Oregon Flame***, a daring rescue . . . a dangerous romance!

Sherry Ann Miller grew up in Long Beach, California, and Pleasant View, Utah. After she met and married her eternal partner, she became the proud mother of seven children and now has twenty-seven grandchildren. Her hobbies include sailing, crabbing, fishing, writing fiction and non-fiction, researching her family history, crocheting, baking, and studying marine life on the beach near her Port Ludlow, Washington, home. Sherry Ann loves to hear from her readers.

Please email her at
sherry@sherryannmiller.com
and be sure to visit her website for sneak peeks of all her novels at
www.sherryannmiller.com